A FICTITIOUS LIFE

PUBLISHED BY THE PISCATIQUA PRESS
AN IMPRINT OF RIVERRUN BOOKSTORE, INC.
142 FLEET STREET | PORTSMOUTH, NH | 03801
WWW.RIVERRUNBOOKSTORE.COM
WWW.PISCATAQUAPRESS.COM

PRINTED IN THE UNITED STATES OF AMERICA

ISBN: 978-1-939739-43-8

A
FICTITIOUS
LIFE

CLAY N.
SAULS

CHAPTER ONE

Walking to Cappy's to visit my girlfriend, I pass the regular slobs on the street. There aren't many today, the heat is probably keeping them indoors. Three scruffy guys wearing dirty loose tank tops and dirty baseball caps walk by talking in loud voices about the way things ought to be done by the city. As if they could run things better. A couple of girls dressed in black from the beauty school sit on the sidewalk in the sun smoking cigarettes. I bet they're hot. An unkempt guy in a brown jacket with epaulets slowly walks by me. It must be 90 degrees and this grimy guy has on a grimy jacket. It's always an unusual walk. At Cappy's, my girlfriend greets me with a smile and a kind hello.

Cappy's is a dingy place, but my girlfriend brightens it up a lot. I never call it Cappy's, I call it Katrina's. She is upbeat and pretty behind the bar today. Katrina doesn't know she is my girlfriend. We have never done anything or gone anywhere together, but I call her my girlfriend anyway. Just not to her. She is my number one fictitious girlfriend. I learned that some girls don't find that stuff very funny. I had another number one, Sophie, but I made the mistake of telling her that I call her my girlfriend and she was not amused. We had a fictitious breakup. I don't want to break up with Katrina, so I won't tell her about our relationship. Unless the beer gets the better of me some day and I make the same mistake I made with my last number one.

My number two girlfriend works out at my gym.

We also greet each other with a smile and kind hello. Linda works out as hard as I do and she is in better shape. She probably has a better diet than I do, but I will never know because she is also a fictitious friend. Number three is my doctor. We only meet on my occasional doctor visits, so we have met four times. She is nice to me and pretty funny, but we are breaking up because she is leaving the practice. Now I won't look forward to checkups. I will still look forward to the gym and the bar. I suppose that means I am fictionally two-timing poor Katrina.

She is quick to serve me and friendly because I over-tip regularly. Fictitious relationships can run into money, for certain. I sometimes think I will look for a different type of relationship, but I don't consider it very seriously. It would take getting to know someone and that would require a lot of talking. It's too much of a commitment. I have nothing against talking itself; it's a pretty good medium for communicating. So many people are so full of shit, though, that talking doesn't seem worth the effort sometimes. When talking to a girl, it's sometimes hard to tell what she is promoting. I'm not ready to listen to someone discuss a subject about which she knows little or even nothing, possibly even less than me. After the big split with Rebecca, I didn't talk to anyone at all for quite a while. I didn't look at girls for longer than that. It took me a really really long time to get to the point where I have fictitious entanglements. Though people began telling me, when I started talking to them again, to date somebody, I couldn't muster the energy to do it. It would take spending time together and I don't think that's such a good idea. If we were able to suffer each other's company, it would lead to promises and obligations even if we didn't say it out loud. I guess I still can't muster the energy. I prefer the fiction.

Unfortunately, Katrina's real boyfriend was in here a couple of weeks ago. He was at the bar with some of his buddies and it was unfortunate because they were obnoxious assholes. Each was loudly and drunkenly boasting about how ferocious he becomes during a fight; each trying to one up the other in his description of his own ferocity. It makes me wonder if I fit the mold for a real relationship with this girl. I know I can be drunk. I know I can be obnoxious. I know I can be ferocious. I don't think those are qualities that I want to brag about. I have a very hard time bragging about myself anyway because it embarrasses me. It also sets a standard for the next incident. If I brag about my fighting skill and tearing someone apart, I had better be able to back it up. I have plenty of shame already, would I want to add to it by bragging about something I can't deliver? I questioned whether the big talkers there had shame. I watched those guys and listened for as long as I could stand it, wondering if I could beat them in the exact situations about which they were so confidently crowing. Could I beat each one? I think I could. It depends upon his training. I have never really had good luck against pros, but I have done pretty well against regular guys. If these guys were just street fighters, I like my chances. Could I take two of them at once? I think I could. Could I beat all of them? I did think and do think I could. I did not like the way that the obnoxious blowing was making me think. I had to get out of there. Fighting is for drunken chumps. Poor Katrina suffered in my tip as well as having those jackasses in her life.

This week it's all better. The patrons are only the regular old guys who live on disability or retirement checks and come for the cheap beer, the camaraderie and to see Katrina. I come for the cheap beer. In fairness, though, visiting with Katrina is my most pleasurable diversion. I try not to get involved with the other people here. I don't want to discuss anything with them, especially the miserable circumstances with which each of these people has to cope. I have my own sob story; I would like to avoid theirs. It has worked out, so far. If the real boyfriend were here, I wouldn't stay. How easy it is for my mind to be taken to dark places when aggression colors the atmosphere. I hope violence is part of my history, not my future. I want it all behind me, but I don't want to be unable to handle it if necessary.

I suppose it's like exercise and fitness. What is the purpose of being fit? I don't play ball any longer, or compete in any sports at all. Is the purpose a longer life? Who thinks that far ahead? How long will I live if I am fit and how long if not fit? If I need to be fit, though, I want to be ready. If my goal is to never fight again, will that make it so? A more important goal is not to be pushed down or slapped around or mugged. What if I have to protect a child or a senior citizen or a girl getting assaulted? I had better be prepared, that's all. The conversation those morons were having when they were here featured a different purpose altogether; a fight to establish manhood, pride or dominance. Those are issues that should be settled during one's youth not so far into maturity. What is most unfortunate of all is that I actually empathize with those obnoxious shitheels. I know what they mean. I feel it. I think I was late to mature and so, like those loudmouths, the issues became settled for me well into adulthood. Well before Rebecca.

CHAPTER TWO

When we first met, I was a different person. Even then, though, I was consciously on a self-improvement program with the goal to be a better man. I have always liked the idea of the Renaissance man. A modern Renaissance man would be athletic, scholarly, generous, trustworthy, wise and patient. As Rebecca and I grew closer and closer, I worked on those qualities. Unfortunately, I was neglecting others that would later turn out to be important; namely, professional, reliable and sober. I guess I'm kind of a flop as a Renaissance man. It looks more like I am closer to idle, ignorant, miserly, irresponsible, foolish and impatient. It's too bad those aren't the qualities that I want to shoot for; I think I could master them pretty easily. Neither one of us knew that though, and before we figured it out, Rebecca was my number one real girlfriend. I felt fulfilled. There were no others for me. Although I was not her number one, I understood and appreciated her freedom. We exercised together and went to bars and restaurants. I recited poetry sometimes and took her on vacations. We were very much alike, I thought. She liked the type of man I was and was trying to become. I look at Katrina and think of the type of man she likes and what he is trying to become. Do I want to be that type? I don't think I do.

I ask about her plans for the weekend with her boyfriend and she tells me they broke up because he was obnoxious and lied about everything. Just like me and Sophie, except a real relationship breakup. And she was not obnoxious and did not lie about anything. If I am forced to admit the truth and make the parallel hold true, Sophie fictitiously dumped me, and for exactly the same reasons that Katrina dumped her obnoxious asshole. When I told her that I called her my girlfriend, I suddenly became an obnoxious asshole who lied. Maybe I am Katrina's type after all. I see the path is open for me to ask Katrina to do something with me. Instead, I stay silent and look around. She moves away to take care of some other duty. I wonder if she wants me to ask, or if asking would be creepy. Does she move away because she wants to avoid the awkward situation an unwelcome invitation would create, or because I am disappointing her by not asking? When I think of asking, I have to think of someplace to go or something to do and, wherever or whatever that is, I don't really want to go there or do that. It would just be her and me. Her company would probably be pretty good. It's the rest that gives me pause. I sometimes forget how much I dislike myself. I am reminded, though, when it comes time for me to make a move; when I contemplate starting a thing with someone. I wonder if she can tell how I feel about me. Can she see into my heart or, even, my head? I hope not. I know what she would see if she had that ability. Probably she can't see in, but how does anyone know what someone else perceives? I wonder what she would decide I feel. I wonder if she has already decided.

I have heard that the eyes are windows to the soul, so it may be possible to analyze someone's soul by looking at his or her eyes enough. I have looked at Katrina's eyes as much as possible and I can't tell anything about her soul. Maybe I lack the gift because I couldn't tell anything about Rebecca from looking at her eyes either, and I was with her for quite a while. If one could read things in another's eyes, hers would be the ones. Her eyes were big, open and clear like the ocean or the sky. She had the ability to stare at me without expression and it was like looking into the universe, into infinity. I never saw her soul or, as it turns out, understood her either. Maybe I am simply imperceptive and unfeeling. If I couldn't read through those eyes, I don't have a shot at reading through anybody's eyes at all. I wonder if other people could see her soul through her eyes. I wonder what new partner is analyzing her soul now.

Pauly is a few spots down the bar. We are fictitious acquaintances. I know his name is Pauly because a couple of the other guys have called to him in the past. We have never spoken to each other. I don't have to look into his eyes to know that he is agitated. Based on his loud complaints, he is upset because his roommate keeps borrowing cigarettes and never pays for any. I suspect that Pauly wants attention, mostly from Katrina. More than attention, I think he wants to borrow cigarettes from her due to her kind heart and his victimization. Depending upon how close a friend he is, he might get them. I wonder if he expects someone to spot him a drink as well. If I am lucky, I will never have a conversation with Pauly. I bet he has a black and greedy soul. Rather than in the eyes, I lean toward the theory that what someone feels is exhibited in external cues like facial expressions, tone of voice and other movements, not necessarily what she or he says. Based on this theory, Pauly wants handouts. I bet he would panhandle everyone in Cappy's if he could get away with it. With the loud whining, he is focused on Katrina for the handouts and letting the rest of the bar give him sympathy.

She is right there when I am ready for another, very

attentive and gracious in keeping me satisfied. How could I not be so fond of her? She is able to give me attention even in an environment surrounded by a bunch of degenerates getting liquored up. I get to talk to her a little bit, but I don't really have much to share. I like her to talk about her simple activities, like raking her yard or moving her furniture. I mostly like to hear her say my name. I have to keep quiet because, though I don't mind sharing things with her, I don't want to share anything with anybody else. It's easy for me to avoid everyone in this dingy bar, especially when everyone is trying to avoid me. The only one anyone really wants to talk to is Katrina anyway. I would stay a lot longer if she spent all of her time with me, but she has too many people to take care of for that and eventually I have to leave. When I do finally leave, Katrina smiles and asks if she will see me tomorrow. I say I will see her if I am lucky. Leaving indicates the end of my social hour. It was very pleasant. But now is the critical time. Now I have to face the essential question. The only question that has any meaning now and maybe ever did have any meaning: Where do I go from here?

CHAPTER **THREE**

I walk slowly so that I don't weave or stumble or anything. Though it's early for that behavior, the heat has unpredictable effects and I don't want to take any chances. I want to be invisible. Attempting to be invisible is totally undermined by stumbling down the city street. Halfway up the block to my apartment, a scraggly woman asks me if I have any spare change. I guess I am not invisible, even though I am not stumbling. I say no perfunctorily, thinking it is bold and pushy asking a stranger for money. I used to feel kind of cheap and selfish for denying that I had spare change. I would say sorry or make an excuse. I've mostly gotten over that, but not entirely. Now I find it kind of annoying that another person will make me feel a little more guilty and cheap than I already do. Do I look prosperous? Maybe I do. I have some decent clothes from before. In fact, I am sweating through a fancy shirt that Rebecca got me at a fancy shop in the Caribbean. If I was going to ask someone for spare change, I suppose I would ask someone with a shirt like this rather than a stained old rag like most of these wandering wraiths wear.

She got me this fancy shirt in Aruba a while ago. My memory of Aruba is hot and windy, clear and beautiful. It seems like there should be poverty somehow, but I never saw any. I see more destitute people here in a ten minute walk than I saw there in two weeks. Elegance appears in some surprising spots. I mean, there will be an area that seems run down, yet an intimate and romantic place will appear suddenly, the way it happens sometimes in a dream. They are more intimate and romantic for the unexpected appearance of them. There will be a beautiful place located behind a lot that looks to be where you throw your broken washing machine in the middle of the night. Passing by a patchy neglected lot I could feel like an arrogant and overdressed intruder; arriving at the destination I am suddenly the Great Gatsby, expected, welcomed and served in an oasis that is as out of place in that setting as I am. It was a long trip getting to Aruba but worth it for the actual time and the memories. Well, most of the memories.

After some days in anticipation, and spending most of a day in airports and airplanes, we arrived in the sweltering Aruba airport ready to ease into comfort. Encased in the cocoon of filmy crawling travel goop that accumulated on our skin during every stage of travel, we were ready to dash to the shower in our resort and become fresh and clean. It felt as if we had slathered motor oil all over our bodies. She rethought the idea of dashing off, though, when she saw our rental jeep. I thought it was a junk, but I thought that probably all vehicles were. Isn't that what people drive on a tiny isolated island without much of anything? She didn't think so. She went to the rental people and said that the broken down heap was an insult and we were not going to settle for it. The rental people promised us a new jeep later in the evening. The junky jeep was only to get us to the resort. She was dubious, but finally agreed after the most sincere promises from the rental people. She proved her wisdom with this move. We could see the ground through the floorboards of this vehicle, the canvas top that should come up as cover was bent and half tattered, it sounded like the muffler was broken, and it did not have second gear. And I thought this would be OK.

Things were better at the resort. We really were able to ease into comfort and, after the rental company actually delivered a brand new jeep, we had no dark apprehension about our ability to travel around the island. It was dinner at a unique fancy place, drinks at another unique fancy place, the waves at an interesting beach, a cruise to an outlying island next to the main one. We drove our brand new jeep over strange terrain to the barren side of the island, went to another interesting and unique restaurant and went shopping at the bustling port tourist shops. She liked the look of a short sleeve white button down shirt with little green palm trees and we joked that they could be dragon flies or maybe pot plants. It was nice either way and I wore it from the shop to the beachside restaurant. I wear it now. I think my heart moved then and again later in the day when we had a server take our picture on the patio of an open-air bar. That was why we were there.

Well, nothing is perfect and I had difficulty locating the restaurant to which we went that night. It was down some desolate road and hard to locate. She became annoyed that I was driving poorly or making U-turns or searching for the driveway. I became annoyed that she was annoyed with me and so we had an argument. She was beautifully dressed and made up. It took her a lot of time and incredible care to get so nearly perfect. During those few moments, her tears marred the flawless makeup; her joyous voice became shaky with frustration and wrath, and our harmonious walk on a cloud of bliss transformed into an angry standoff in a muddy parking lot. How we resolved our disagreement, I cannot recall. I do recall that, as we had dinner, I wondered about the same thing I wonder about now: What kind of brute could ruin the magic of this beautiful creature in this beautiful place on this beautiful evening? Moments only, though, that were soon swept away by the frequent and fascinating sights and adventures ahead. Dinners, night walks, night swims and professions of devotion seemed to erase any anguish from our spirits. Those moments were not really erased, though. I remember them now.

Anger and dejection returned a couple of days later, though. Anger for her, dejection for me. I was a little disoriented that morning as I drove us across a split 4 lane highway, a strange construction on such a tiny island. As I reached the halfway point in the first 2 lanes, a car came barreling down the road toward us. In some confusion, I stopped our jeep in the road causing the other driver to slam on his brakes. The car smashed into the side of our brand new jeep. It didn't do much to the jeep, but there was a lot of damage to the little car and to my self-esteem. I felt pretty low as the Aruba policeman took information. I chastised myself. How could I have let that happen? Why was I so tentative crossing the road? What was this going to cost? What have I done to the brand new jeep? How does Rebecca feel about this? As she drove us away from the scene in our slightly dented vehicle, I waited for her to ask me all of those questions and more. She never asked any of them, though. In spite of that incident, we resumed having a lovely time. I do wonder what lasting damage the accident caused. I also wonder what damage the argument caused and which caused more damage, the accident or the argument. When we were checking in at the airport getting ready to leave some time later, we nearly missed our plane due to a delay in the paperwork concerning the accident and the insurance coverage. Somehow, the auto coverage information was slow to arrive in Aruba. I don't know the details, but I'm sure that Rebecca does. The final hours of our stay in Aruba were consumed with contention over my accident and worry over missing our flight home. It was not the way I would choose to end our trip to paradise. Of all of the beautiful and timeless moments during those days, the moments of anger in that dirt lot in front of a gem in the wilderness are the most poignant.

I wonder what she remembers most about that trip. Does she remember walking together in the clean, perfect sand under a cloudless blue sky? Or dining at a place on a beach where we could put our feet in the water without leaving our table if we chose? Does she remember swimming together in clear, warm ocean water as pelicans dove from the sky and crashed into the water nearby to get fish? Or me holding her above the crests of the waves as they tried to take us toward the beach? Does she remember marveling at the swans in a dining room lagoon or the view during lunch from the lighthouse overlooking the ocean to the south? Does she instead remember my foolish indecision that caused an accident and inconvenience, if not quite a disaster? My deepest desire and greatest hope is that she does not remember crying in a parking lot on what started out as a perfect night. I hope she does not remember the tears I caused in ignorance. I hope that I carry that burden all by myself. I think I needed only the wisdom to soothe her during a moment of anxiety, and I failed. Did that ruin the perfect time together, or did it ruin everything? I can only wonder about it now.

CHAPTER FOUR

When I approach my building, I don't want to go in there. The idea of being inside right now makes me feel pent up, confined. Instead, I walk to a bench next to the brand new canal-walk the city built last year. I know the city isn't through with this project, but it is through with this corner. I can sit here and smoke while I sweat and hope nobody passes by. Some people always pass by nowadays, though. A year ago, this part of the canal-walk was still under construction and nobody came by here. Now I have to try to make believe that I don't see them and hope they don't see me. Of course, my hope is dashed when a guy asks me for a cigarette. I say no.

I still feel kind of funny about smoking. I'm a secret smoker. I try to do it when no one is around and where nobody can see me. It is solitary operation not a social one and I try to keep it secret. I've given it some thought and have decided that it's a form of masturbation and I sure don't want to share that. Unlike regular masturbation, smoking seems like a useless and dumb thing to do, I think as a suck down some smoke. It makes everything smell, gets ashes everywhere and gives everyone cancer. It gives me no pleasure, instead it gives me bad breath and I always feel a little guilty when doing it; like I'm doing something wrong. I want to say I am just acting in protest against all of the things blamed on smoking and second hand smoke, like cancer, emphysema, hair loss, skin rash, hang nails, crossed eyes, limping and all manner of things. I find that so irritating that I would like to say that I smoke just to prove a point. It isn't true, though.

I began to smoke gradually. It seems to have reflected the state of my relationship with her. I didn't know that we were growing distant; that is, there was nothing that I could point out specifically. I guess I could sense it on some level but I think I hoped I was mistaken. There was nothing I could do about it except, I guess, make it worse by being myself. I would smoke one with her when she went outside to do it. It was something to do together. Then I would smoke another one here and one there. All the while, she was less and less happy with me, with us. Although she smoked, she showed signs of disdain when I did it. Apparently, the more I smoked, the more disdain she felt for me. Somewhere along the way, I began to associate smoking with us. If I stop smoking now, will the relationship then be over? Is it not completely over yet because I am smoking? No. It's all over now except for the smoking.

The bench is a pretty good place for contemplation. Maybe too good. Time can get away from me, sitting here watching the canal-walk the city constructed and the trees the city planted. In good weather, the park service gives tours on those canals. When a tour boat passes by, the tourists are only about 10 feet away. I go somewhere else. Who wants to take a historic tour and see some tramp sitting there smoking in the middle of it? As the tour putters by, I stroll over to a remote part of the canal embankment where no tours pass. It is private enough that I take off my shirt and sit on an old broken stone bridge support. It is interesting how all of these broken pieces of the city have charm. They each have a story and are imbued with the history of their construction and former purpose. Each was important during its time and had its specific use. It was an important part of the city once, welcomed and loved for what it gave. When that part of city grew or shrank or moved or evolved, the piece was abandoned and ignored. It watched other things become important while it just sat there, unwanted. The city turned its back on the piece and focused on a new, more interesting item. And now the piece sits there, broken. After all of this time, the piece has caught the attention of the city once more, a different faction in charge. The old faction now a part of the past and the new faction interested in the lonely piece of construction that at one time held an important or interesting place in the city. Now it has charm again, after so much time was wasted and lost. Now it, along with so many other pieces, will be reclaimed, reconstructed and put to use, valuable in some way once more.

Behind me, somebody says hello startling me a little. Damn, another shitbum asking me for a cigarette. When I look around, irritated, I find that am wrong. It's a park ranger. Hi. Have I done something or am I doing something wrong? Am I not supposed to be here? She asks if I live there. Huh? As I sit there with no shirt, I tell her that I do live here, in that building right there. She is actually asking me if I live there on the canal under the foot bridge. After I point out where I live and tell her what I am doing, she explains that some bums do stay under that bridge and others on the canal. She tells me it is OK to be there, but the city doesn't want people living down here on the canal. Apparently, it makes the canal tours less attractive, though probably a little more interesting. She tells me to be careful when I am hanging around there because some guys live right there where I am. They leave trash, used needles and feces all around the place there. Have a nice day,

Bye. Looking around the ground I see some trash, but I don't see any needles and feces. I do believe the ranger anyway. I guess I won't frolic in the grass around here. I know this city a little bit more intimately than I did before. The private spot on the canal is no longer attractive to me.

Is this my city now? I live here, I walk it, I see it more closely than most I'll bet. Does that make it my city? How many people who live here, work here or come here for other things have seen it so closely? Those homeless people have seen it that closely, I know, but what about all of the others? When you meet a guy in Hampton, Philadelphia or New Orleans and he says he is from Lowell, does he know what the city really looks like? Does he know about the needles and feces on the canal?

I sometimes walk by the canals, look in them and see the water sitting there, like today, mostly idle. That means that the locks are closed farther down the canal and the water is stuck in place, with broken things down there in it. When the locks are open, the water will run like a river. The level changes every day, depending on when and where the water is released. Sometimes I can only see the water, dark, angry maybe a little sinister. Does it dare someone to touch it or even go into it? Sometimes the water level is low enough that I can see a shopping cart, a bicycle, a refrigerator door, some car tires. The canal is a river, but one that has been trapped, bullied, exploited and abused until it has developed a resentful petty cruelty. The Merrimack River that feeds the canals, though also exploited and trapped, runs kind of freely in its own banks. It's less sneaky but still angry. The river doesn't seem to have the frustrated anger of a canal but a contemptuous vitality. It has been around for so long, travelling its own course that some people forget the dangerous anger it contains. Also slightly abused, it gets its revenge from time to time. It cuts the city in two and sometimes when there is a lot of rain, it will overflow, flooding the condominiums and schools built near its banks; something the canals would never be able to do. Every now and then, a boater will go swimming in the Merrimack and the river will take him, kill him and deposit his corpse on the bank somewhere farther down the river. Even though they are filled with the same water, the canals are too young and obvious for anyone to go in, unless it's a drunken accident, or an immigrant from somewhere with places even more dark and polluted than an inner city pseudo-dump. The canals could never get the satisfaction that the river gets by murdering some dumbass who goes in for a drunken recreational swim.

Maybe this isn't my city, maybe I belong to it. With dark veins running through it, dangerous and mysterious, the dirty and neglected edges, hidden and foul, even the attempts at self-improvement trying to move the city closer to the place it would like to be. There are spots that the city does not examine too closely just yet. The city will probably get to them later, when it has time or if the money doesn't run out, after it fixes up some of the other trouble spots. I wonder how I landed in a place that I identify with so closely. Was I pushed here by a cosmic energy that forces like things together? Or maybe drawn here like a broken shard of metal to a magnet? It certainly was not a goal of mine or part of a specific long term plan. I somehow just stumbled around and came to rest here.

CHAPTER FIVE

When she sent me away from home, I stayed for a time in that vacant apartment in nearby Dracut. It was the worst and the best situation imaginable and I sometimes wonder how I survived it. How did I even live it? I was lucky to be able to stay there. Somehow, God and Wade arranged it so that I had the place to myself. I was not on someone's couch or sharing a space with another sad sack. I was mercifully alone. There were a couple of empty bedrooms, an empty living room, an empty kitchen and bathroom. A bed. It was as if it had been prepared beforehand and was just waiting for me. I moved into the place with my glasses and toothbrush in a little bag on the passenger's seat of my car. I moved out with clothes, papers, books, pictures, boxes and dishes; everything I had accumulated in all of our time together. Everything I had accumulated in my whole life. I went there for a couple of nights to give her the time to realize how much she missed and needed me. I put the beach chair from the trunk of my car on the hardwood floor of the living room and I sat there, self-righteous, indignant and angry, waiting for her to come to her senses and call me back. She said she needed some time when she asked me to leave. Like she planned to clear her mind and think of ways that would make everything right again. At first, I didn't believe it. After a while, though, I said Fine. I would give her all of the time she wanted. Arrogantly, I asked her how many times that made a relationship work out. I couldn't think of any. I did not like it, but she could have her time. Though I didn't say it, I felt that she could damned well call me in a couple of days and ask me back, with contrition. It didn't work out exactly as I expected. Is it possible that she had already ended us?

I put my shirt on. It might be a little late for that since I already finished talking to the park ranger. If I was wearing the shirt, maybe she would not have thought I was a homeless bum living under the bridge. Or maybe she would have asked me for a cigarette. Sirens begin to wail in the distance. There are sirens here pretty often. I still can never tell if a siren belongs to a police car, an ambulance or a fire truck. I don't think it matters because at every emergency, there's a police car, ambulance and fire truck anyway. That means that every incident includes a broken law, an injury and a fire. I suppose it could happen that way in this part of the city, with the old folk's home two blocks away and the homeless shelter one block away. I can see the old folks needing an ambulance if one of them broke a hip up on the sixth floor of that home and needing a fire truck if he or she knocked over a space heater or something during the fall. I don't know what the police would do. Maybe keep an eye out so the firemen that showed up didn't steal the old folk's wallet. It is possible at the homeless shelter because that houses the drug addicts and drunks who can't pay rent. They are the ones who spend all of their money on the drugs and the booze that make them mindless and out of control. One of the drunks could slurp up something ninety proof and ignite himself trying to light a cigarette in the shelter. That would call for an ambulance, fire truck and the police. Usually, though, all of those emergency responders seem excessive. The city is so broke that the schools can't afford to have gym class for the kids but an army of firemen get paid to show up at a barroom brawl. There was no fire and so no need at all for the fire truck when one showed up at CC's at two thirty in the morning.

Nine of us went to CC's nightclub and shithole. We had spent the day playing softball, drinking beer and snorting cocaine. Our softball team wasn't bad and we liked to hang out together after the games. CC's was a nightclub because it was a big place with dark lighting, black lights in some spots, loud music, a dance area and cocktail waitresses that wore fishnet stockings with their little spandex uniforms. It was a shithole because it was cheap enough that anyone could afford it, they let anybody in and there was carpeting covering a lot of the floor. It was pretty popular and you could count on someone in the place puking on the carpet every weekend. I would not like to see that place in the light. A couple of the guys from my team danced with some girls. I think they were better at softball, but I wasn't dancing with them. I was following little Lisle around. Even with braces she was especially cute. Maybe that was because of the bourbon and cocaine I had ingested. Or maybe it was because of the fishnet stockings she wore as the lower part of her spandex outfit. The other guys did their separate things to try and meet girls, like playing some video games out back or dancing, if you can call what they were doing dancing, while I talked with Lisle and proved that I was cool.

Lisle and I were getting along really well, we always did. The costume might make her job serving cocktails look like sexual exploitation but she knew what she wanted and was not shy about getting it. Exhibitionism paid, plus it was an innocent pleasure that she would not deny herself. She was surprisingly idealistic for a girl in a skimpy Vampirella outfit surrounded by leering jackals night after night. Though she worked in that raucous environment with all of the energy and emotion and jealousy swirling around, she would not keep company with any violent types. There were fights at CC's from time to time and Lisle always criticized anyone who participated. She said you could always have a fun time without any violent confrontation and violence was opposed to what the place was about and what she was about. Love not war and all of that. CC's seemed like a strange place to be a pacifist. It seemed to me that the place was about arm wrestling and competing for girls and getting drunk. I didn't know much about Lisle's family or history or anything but I knew she was a pacifist and an energetic server who made pretty good money there. She was a pretty wild pacifist; that was really all I needed to know.

The first time I met her was at CC's the night she took me to her townhouse. With her belt coiled around her wrists, she stretched her arms above her head and ran it through the rails of the headboard while she rolled onto her stomach to display the seams on her stockings. They ran from the high heels she wore all the way to her waist beneath the bottom part of her leotard uniform. I had to fight with her uniform and ended up destroying her fishnet stockings. The violence I committed against her outfit made Lisle quiver with a violence of her own. She wanted it to wash over her and dominate her, the rougher, the better. Her enthusiasm enthralled me and put me under a spell. Lisle was not the first pacifist I had ever met. She wasn't the first masochist I had ever met, either. But she was the first masochist pacifist who craved bondage and sodomy that I had ever heard of. I didn't even know there was such a thing. I guess she believed in keeping violence in the home. She liked the guys who went to CC's but didn't like the things they did there. She liked me because I was not afraid of the rough and wild environment but didn't participate in the roughness. That was probably because I seldom went there with a bunch of guys. Or because Lisle would not have put up with it. Plus, I was very complimentary of her work uniform.

I was not the only one in my group who was having good luck that night. Our right fielder, Tony, was having good luck, too, but it would not be lucky for the rest of us. He had met a girl who was going to take him to her apartment, but the guy she had come with objected. I didn't know anything about Tony's luck when, towards the end of the night, another one of our group found me and told me to go outside and see what was going on. Since Lisle was busy working, I had plenty of time to go out to the front of CC's and check it out. She had come up with a plan for me when she was finished with work. The plan was for me to go home with her and discuss the violent nature of pacifism. It was a good plan. When I went out the front door, that plan suddenly changed. Standing there without a shirt a few feet from the door was our left fielder Trey telling another guy, also without a shirt, that the only thing between them was air and opportunity. There must have been 200 people milling around, some watching Trey, some watching each other. The walkway and parking area were full of people, mostly angry looking. I didn't know how one bar could hold so many people. The van we drove to the bar was so close that I could have hit it with a beer. It was right there on the street. I could have rescued my excellent plan if I had rushed in, grabbed Trey low and used our momentum to carry us to the van and into it, except the door wasn't open yet. Center fielder Joe was on the curb next to the van and he wasn't the type to become embroiled in the building storm. I went over to get him to open the side door and, since it looked like a violent situation was developing, I had him hold onto the cocaine I had in my pocket. I should have just gotten into the van. My attention was caught by our small second baseman Benny, as he mouthed off a short distance away to some large guys who looked at him without smiles. Right fielder Tony was nowhere to be seen. It turns out that by that time, he was already at a girl's apartment talking about peace and love, not softball and bar brawls.

Lisle would have been proud of the way I went over to little Benny and got him out of the situation with the group of large guys. That was me, diffusing the situation. Benny was really telling them off. He was too small for them to do anything about, but I wasn't. When I corralled him and began to take him toward our van with both arms wrapped around him, I glibly told the big hairy guys Benny was chewing out that I had him under control and everybody could fuck off and go away. One of the hairy men hit me in the face so hard that I didn't feel the next couple of shots he gave me. Benny told me about it later. I regained my senses soon enough to hear police sirens in the distance and I figured we had to get away from there. Unfortunately, one of the big guys hit me again. Fortunately, I had already taken the first one, or three, and was not taken by surprise. I had regained awareness by then and was not as damaged as energized. I was able to let go of Benny, turn my body to avoid the fist that could have probably knocked me out again and hit the guy who tried to hit me. The fucker had a hairy beard that absorbed some of my power so he didn't fall down. He did have the audacity to look surprised that I punched him in the jaw. I assumed that he was together with the crowd of enemies who were all looking to punish my team. As he staggered back, I jumped into the angry looking circle of men who probably didn't even know each other. I punched a guy with a cocked arm in the neck and he dropped like a sack as I turned to hit another asshole and then another. The truth is that I didn't know who I was hitting, but somebody was hitting me in the back of the head and if I hit enough guys, I was bound to hit the right one. I moved my head enough to avoid direct blows and wheeled on somebody. I assumed it was an assailant and with so many people swinging at me I could not have been wrong. I struck a guy with my fist hard enough to make him go away. For all I knew, it could have been my brother, but we were outnumbered and I could not let my guard down. At least I was outnumbered; Benny had disappeared in the melee. I made my way to the van on the street while unsuccessfully dodging fists and taking some kicks. For each hit and kick, I tried to give at least one strike to whichever person I saw near me. I couldn't tell if I hit the right guy, but I hit somebody.

The mass of people hitting me began to disperse and I was able to get into our van before I lost a limb or something. The police had arrived with a couple of fire trucks and an ambulance. That explained the thinning of the mob trying to kick my ass. The spinning lights from a handful of emergency vehicles came from the street some way behind us and we were able to maneuver the van through some of the milling people and drive away before the cops got hold of us. At least some of us got away because there were only five of us in the van when we left. The three we left behind were questioned but not injured or arrested. We thought we had left four, but Tony was already gone. They told us later that a couple of people were taken away in the ambulance and some others were taken away in police cars. The cops couldn't find the one person they were really looking for. It was the guy who was fighting with a mob. He was last seen making his way toward the street while punching a girl who was holding onto his waist. Right fielder Tony didn't tell us anything informative. I have not yet figured out what the fire trucks did that night.

I had to rest up for a few days after that night out with the softball team. They turned out to be a hard partying group. I had some lumps on the back and sides of my head and bruises on most of my body. It wasn't until the next week that I went back to CC's to see Lisle. I hoped no one would recognize me. I figured it wasn't likely, since the brawl from the week before was outside and mostly in the dark. There were so many people out there that any one guy was probably indistinguishable from any other. On the other hand, there were so many people out there that someone was bound to recognize me from that mess and, sure enough, someone did: Lisle. It wasn't hard for her to avoid me that night in a place that size filled with that many people. I had a hard time catching up with her so she could break up with me. When I finally cornered her at one of those service areas where she had to go in order to get drinks, she told me that I was a week late in seeing her and she was too busy for me now. I said I would wait. She looked me straight in the eye, the black one, and told me not to wait because she was too busy for me later, too. She did take the time to explain that she saw me outside fighting last week and if there was one thing she could not stand, it was somebody fighting especially at her place of employment. In general, she did not like street brawlers punching each other outside a bar. She again explained her stance on violence and how I had disappointed her with my behavior and how she could not spend time with someone like that. I stood there, in that rowdy crowded shithole where violence often erupted, surrounded by aggressive young drunks, and I got dumped by a masochist for hurting someone. Simultaneously, I got dumped by a pacifist who was dressed for torture, and there was no doubt she had violence planned for later. I tried to explain that the circumstances were beyond my control, but Lisle would not hear it. In her mind, it was the fact that I was out there fighting, not how it came about. It showed a lack of respect for her that she could not accept. Was I supposed to be some kind of boyfriend or something; outside fighting where she worked? How embarrassing. My complete abandon in that madness proved that I lacked self-control. Had I no restraint? How could she trust someone like that? How would she know that I wouldn't end up hitting her when she did something I didn't like? I didn't have a very good defense against her reasoning. I mean, everything she said made a crooked kind of sense. I didn't point out that I had hit her plenty of times and it was always when she was doing something I liked.

I guess she really was a pacifist because she stood by what she said. It was frustrating because I had to go into that environment to see her and yet that environment encouraged the very behavior that she could not accept. I knew there would be another fight at CC's, maybe even that night. It happened so often that the cops arrived before 200 people could beat my ass. I was powerless to persuade her to understand my side and keep seeing me because everything she said was logical and correct. But her actions seemed contradictory to her logic. She did not see a contradiction in refusing to accept that I beat some guys in self-defense, yet demanding that I beat her in passion. I wondered if she could explain her views on violence against women, but I would never get the chance to hear them because Lisle made it clear that she was finished with my violence. Maybe I should have ignored my teammates' situations and gone straight to our van when I got outside the week before. Even better, I should never have gone to CC's with other guys. I would have to plan things better in the future. My new plans could start right away because I was alone. My frustration made me want to attack the fishnet stockings that Lisle wore, but I could not do that anymore. She was gone.

CHAPTER SIX

I can hear the sirens and see the flashing lights in the distance over the canals. It is a fire truck this time. I can only see the top of it over the barriers that line the street. I wonder about what kind of situation could require the emergency response of a fire truck. It should be an emergency, because if it's not, the truck shouldn't have the sirens blaring and lights flashing. I am not convinced. I think it's probably fake. It's probably just a joy ride for the firemen who like the siren. There was a real emergency down the street a couple of months ago. Somebody in one of those weekly-rental apartments was cooking on a hot-plate or lighting a candle or smoking in bed in the middle of the day. The threadbare curtains in his dumpy apartment caught fire. It spread to the next dumpy apartment and pretty soon, the top floor of the three-story apartment building was on fire. Smoke sort of saturated half of the city. There must have been thirty fire trucks covering that fire. That kind of conflagration is a pretty rare occurrence these days, though. With all of the building codes, fire regulations, smoking bans, alarms, warnings and extinguishers of all types located in public places, fires like that don't happen very often. The fire truck might be going to a false alarm. That happens quite a bit. There are false alarms a couple of times a week in the building next door to my apartment. A real fire would be pretty interesting. A false alarm is about as interesting as one of those stiffs at Katrina's talking about what he's going to do when his check comes in. I would rather avoid the clamor of the sirens and the attention demanded by the lights. I suppose it's possible that one of the people coming out of the train station up the street got hit by a car and all of the other emergency vehicles are there already. That qualifies as an emergency, I guess. At least to the person who got hit. It isn't likely, though. It's just another attention grabbing hoax. I find the abandoned bridge support that I sit on more interesting. At least it really did something once.

My mind wanders around a little bit. I appreciate that. For a time it didn't do anything, as if it was imprisoned by one of those evil sorcerers that always attack Hogwart's, the school for wizards in the book about magic kids. More like it was tranquilized or overdosed and went into a coma. When I look back from here it's odd, almost hard to imagine, that for so long I thought of only one thing. While staying at the place in Dracut, it kept me busy. I sat in the beach chair or went to the bathroom or walked the streets opening or gripping or glancing at my durable and obsolete cellular flip-phone. I walked around in the yard with my phone in my hand. The yard I paced had a privacy fence. There wasn't total privacy, though, because I shared it with the people living in the apartment adjoining the one I occupied. I didn't want to talk to them because I was busy with the phone. I tried with moderate success to avoid them and their questions. I lay on the bed with the phone. She didn't call me that day. I don't know how I slept or if I did. I know I got up though. I went back to the chair. I walked up the block and sat in the baseball field. I lay on the bed. She didn't call that day. I went to the chair and she didn't call. I walked around the yard and she didn't call. At the field, she did not call. I figured that my phone might be broken, so I called the drug store. The phone worked fine which caused me to grow a little confused, a little anxious. If my phone wasn't broken, then what was?

It couldn't be us. We had a partnership for life. I thought the idea of a life partnership was to work on things and fix what is wrong. The whole point being to hook arms with the person we have chosen as a love, ally and partner and to fight through the hard times. Defeat the forces aligned against us. I chose her and she chose me. They can't win because we have each other. We have love. We made vows that bound us closer than anyone ever in the whole world and ever in eternity. We promised. What the hell was I doing in an empty apartment alone on a beach chair? When we got to the working-it-out part, she could explain it to me. She could admit her guilt in this, but I would not be very hard on her. She was probably confused or something. When she told me what I had done and what I could do to make everything better for good, I would do it and this trouble would all be over. I would be generous, forgiving, Renaissance-man like and we would live happily ever after.

After some days, I decided I needed more than my glasses and toothbrush. What I thought I needed, I don't know, since I didn't need very much sitting resentfully and now confusedly in the beach chair in the empty living room or pacing around outside, thinking and sweating, sometimes reading, always holding the phone and waiting for the call. I guess I wanted to check up on our house and see what signs of loneliness were left out in the open. Maybe I just missed her. I went home during a time I knew she would not be there because I didn't want to seem weak to her, or even worse, lonely without her. I didn't see many signs of loneliness or sadness in our house. None in fact. The place was as neat and tidy as ever. It was cool with air conditioning and clean. There were no signs that she missed me, but they would be very hard to notice when the house was so well kept. It was a little disappointing, but at least the place wasn't getting seedy. I couldn't really expect a shrine. It was too soon for that, probably. Though I wanted to stay, I got a few things in a bag before she returned and went back to the apartment to wait for her call.

Going home had made me inexplicably more hopeful and impatient. She didn't call me that day, or any day after that one. The phone became my sole concern. I couldn't think of eating or drinking. Reading was impossible. Showering became the central dreadful focus of each day. Lying down was no different than sitting in the chair or walking in the yard. With the arrival of each day, each one delivering an increment of doubt, my righteous anger lessened a little and my confused anxiety increased. My loneliness increased, too. I wanted to talk about it, but only with her. What kind of conversation it would be, I didn't know because I didn't practice anything to say. I had only questions. I became more enervated by the day. When enough days or weeks or months had come, victimization was surpassed by guilt, and indignation was surpassed by loneliness. But I couldn't figure out what I was guilty of. After lying or sitting or standing day after day, clinging to my phone, I began to acquire a whole new emotion: despair. I didn't know what it was, but I knew it was something vastly different. I figured that maybe worms were eating my insides, or ants. After plenty more days or years or centuries of acquiring my new emotion, on another day like all of the others, each one like rolling in burning chunks of broken glass, and when the resentment was so small that I couldn't find it, I succumbed to desperation and did what I had set out not to do but couldn't remember why: I called her. Call me weak. Was some of it a dream? All of it?

CHAPTER SEVEN

Looking the ground over some more, I still don't see any needles or feces. I don't want to look any more closely. I will leave this ground to the homeless. I walk over the expanse of empty pavement that separates the canal from the fence of a parking lot. It is adjacent to a large empty building lot on one side. Some long gone factory used to occupy that lot. Now people take their dogs out there to shit because nobody makes them pick it up. In the front of my apartment building, they are required to pick up their dog poop, though some people don't do it. There are signs in the lobby of my building instructing pet owners to clean up after their pets. Some people like to exercise their individual rights by not picking up their dog's crap on the lawn. On the other side of me is a moderately sized grassy area with the new canal-walk and some benches on the far side. It is like a lawn or play area where many people take their dogs to gambol and play Frisbee. At this moment, a couple of people are lying on the grass getting sun I think. I am not certain, but I think it is a homeless man wooing a homeless woman with a picnic lunch of mini bottle nips of liquor. I don't think I would lie around there because I am certain that many of the same people who do not pick up their dog shit in front of my apartment building do not pick up their dog shit on that grassy expanse. That romantic devil is showing his sweetheart a good time, though.

It isn't the first time I have seen one of those guys romancing someone right around that spot there near the benches. I wonder somewhat about the relationship. Is he trying to pick up a new girl, or is it his long-term relationship? Is he trying to be a playboy, an unwashed derelict version of one, or is he doing his poor best during hard times to give his love a small amount of pleasure? Proud dirty stud or faithful honest partner? Ludicrous or sympathetic? The nips of booze in the park make me lean toward the ludicrous. Which one is better, anyway? The playboy approach seems like a better option at first. A lot of guys make a really strong argument for the playboy life. The faithful honest partner, though, seems like a more honorable and honest approach. But if a guy says he's a playboy, he can't be a cheater no matter how many times he steps out. Because he said he was going to cheat beforehand, he isn't a liar when he does. It is more a dream than a life, really. Every guy wishes he were so desirable that all women found him irresistible. If he pretends that he is a faithful honest partner and he steps out one time, even if it's the only time any woman actually does find him desirable, he becomes a liar. Apparently, any guy can be either one or the other no matter what his financial or domestic circumstances; he just has to change his target audience. We are all so much the same all of the time in every situation until someone brings the hammer down. Then maybe we are different for a very short time. Ludicrous. From the richest to the poorest, the behavior is the same; the only thing that differs is the setting. And maybe the hygiene. I learned my lesson, I swear I did. But I suspect, OK, I know, it is only until the next time.

I wonder what made me think that I would be such a good partner when I had so much evidence that I would somehow undermine the whole thing. I had the notion that it would be different this time because the two of us were so compatible, so alike, so perfect together that we could so figure anything out. I set out to be the best partner ever, the perfect one. My previous perfect partnership taught me some of the things to avoid in order to keep the love strong. Entering that one, I had it figured out and I knew what was what. I planned on going into it with Lucy strong and confident. I would be my own man and let her do her own thing. I would be in control this time. I would be in charge of my destiny and provide her with fun and good times. But I knew even at the very beginning that it was a false attitude. When I entered that relationship I was already being sneaky.

She was one together girl. Lucy and I did not live together in the early days. I was certain that she had some other boyfriend taking her out when she began dating me because she was too sexy for one guy. She would come to visit and we would go out. Or she would come to visit and we would stay in. Her long black hair was naturally curly and attention grabbing while the rest of her was riveting. I would take her to dinner at the Oarhouse and watch the waiter try not to stare at her, but then stare anyway when he thought I wasn't looking. We would go to the Pressroom for a beer and the drunkards would ogle as she walked through to the bathroom. Lucy did not get drunk. During a celebration at Molly's, a group of guys encircled her to listen with rapt attention as she chatted with them. One of the guys would engage her in very interesting conversation as the others tried to see down her shirt and jacket or look up her short skirt, depending on the angle. She, like everyone else in the place, was fully aware of the game being played on her but she had too much style to be rude or cause a scene. I, on the other hand, like the guys trying to get a beaver shot, lacked the grace to be as cool as Lucy. After I watched the display for as long as I could stand, I bullied my way through the little circle to her side and drunkenly challenged those licentious bastards. The collective wit of those assholes was better than mine, I'm sure, but my courage and anger was certainly stronger. I expect none of us looked too good in the name calling shoving match that ensued, with the exception of Lucy. When the bouncers and helpful onlookers got everyone separated and quieted, she was still sitting just where she had been since the beginning. While we talked about the incident and our different views on it, I listened to her with rapt attention. I was smooth and cool as I stood there next to her beautiful legs and subtly tried to look up her short skirt.

I had some pretty good street credibility while with Lucy. My skills with women could only be wondered at by everyone around me. They all figured I must be something pretty special to have such an incredible girlfriend and the longer we were together, the more respect I gained. She would still come over and we would do whatever I chose for that visit because her errands or duties were already done for the day. I looked commanding and worldly in addition to having a special gift in the ability to satisfy the most desirable of women. I must have been great company and an exceptional lover. The girl in the apartment above me and her friends were pretty shy and respectful toward both Lucy and me. She was cute, but not a beauty like Lucy and she knew that. On a random sunny day when Lucy was not visiting, Sherry from above and I were both in the yard doing our respective chores and wearing whatever revealing outfits the weather permitted. We talked about not much and she shyly watched me do not much. I boldly admired her while deigning to show interest in whatever she had to say. Before we eventually went up to her apartment for water, she had already surrendered to me. I knew it and she knew I knew it, so there was not much preliminary small talk or anything.

I felt desirable and right as I betrayed my girlfriend, while Sherry was honored and eager. I wonder if a betrayal becomes more egregious if it stretches out over a long period of time. It seems that a sin is magnified if it could be over quickly but is purposely extended longer and longer. If the deceiver happily wallows in his debauchery, flaunting the satisfaction of desire with a mostly innocent, if willing, quarry, isn't that the most heinous of acts? I didn't quickly rush into an illicit mistake and guiltily slink back to my own apartment. I knew how girls were. Look how I was able to read Sherry and give her what she most wanted. I was like some middle school molester; one of those gym teachers who takes advantage of his position. Sherry didn't stand a chance. And Lucy? Lucy was too beautiful and sexy for someone with questionable morality to comprehend. I figured that she had certainly been doing the same thing with someone. She had to have been. There was no question. Too many guys and a few girls hit on her for her to be faithful to me. I was lascivious, abandoned and free until Sherry had to do something else some time the next day. I smiled all day as I created justifications for a wholly inexcusable treachery. I probably would not have been smiling so much had I understood the way in which I had betrayed everyone. It wasn't so much that I actually did it. That was bad enough, but it could probably be considered a human weakness. It may not even be surprising in the circumstances, since the two of us were isolated together with mutual curiosity and attraction. The deeper betrayal was my disingenuous approach to the whole affair. In addition, my utter abandon while engaged in duplicity and my blithe attitude afterward created an ugliness out of something that may not have been so bad. The way I conducted myself was an insult to Lucy, Sherry and me.

There was no confusion or mystery in what went wrong with that relationship. Lucy was beautiful, yes, but she was also honest and faithful. She was not promiscuous, I was. So many people wanted to seduce her because she had so many of the qualities that we all most admire in another human. She was honest. She was true. She was hard-working, smart and demure. She was independent and self-possessed, yet humble. When she was insulted, she did not make a scene. She let it be known with dignity. When she was praised, she did not overreact. She let her appreciation be known without fanfare. She had a right to expect that the person to whom she was closest would keep her integrity and trust in mind. That person should be expected not to sully her image, but to remember her dignity and honorable qualities. Instead, that person scoffed at her integrity and betrayed her trust. He soiled her image by assuming she had no dignity or honor. Of course, she knew nothing of the horrible destruction of her character by me. Unbeknownst to Lucy, I had invented a fictitious lover for her. I had also undermined the admiration Sherry and her friends felt for Lucy and me. Sherry had looked upon us as a couple that should be emulated and me as a figure worthy of respect. After my treatment, she saw Lucy either as a libertine or a dupe. She had to figure out if Lucy was immoral enough to approve when her boyfriend, me, performed such intimate perversions with another, her, or if Lucy was just ignorant. She saw me as a seducer who could not be trusted with a girl's virtue; a selfish glutton without shame. Maybe she was right. It looked like I could come up with a justification for any unsavory act I wanted to perpetrate. In the end, I had also betrayed myself in creating a Lucy who was not real. I had cheapened her in my mind and had thereby lost everything good that she was. Except, of course, the beautiful wanton.

CHAPTER EIGHT

I look away from the love scene on the grass and make my way up the paved slope toward the street. A couple of people come toward me on the walk path, so I head to the right in order that I don't pass them. I make a big circle. They look determined, like they have some place important to go. I do too since the beer I drank is now demanding my attention and I have to find a place to go pee. All of the public bathrooms are inside of something. If I go into a store, I will have to pretend to shop; go into a bar, I will have to buy a beer. The grocery store is too far and so are the library and my apartment by now. I look around to see if there are any hiding places nearby where no one can see me while I secretly do it. The problems with urinating outside in the city are that pedestrians walk by, canal boats float by, people drive by, apartment windows look down, it is unsanitary and I don't know if it's against the law or not. I have never seen anyone do it, but I know they do. I have walked down a couple of the streets near here that smell more like piss than the giant toilets at Fenway Park. Since I have doubts about my invisibility, some caution is in order. I have been working very hard at being invisible, but I guess I'm no good at it since somebody asks for money or cigarettes every time I go out.

Really, though, being invisible mostly depends on where I am and who is looking. It seems that places like the malls, the stores, the movies, the bars, the restaurants or anywhere regular people go to do regular things, like throw around bunches of money, nobody sees me at all. I am easy to overlook nowadays. The other places like the city benches on the canals, the city parks during odd times of the day, the poor parts of town and anywhere else the less fortunate people go to avoid wasting or even spending any money, everybody sees me just fine. The affluent see nothing valuable about me and I could disappear, maybe I already have. The homeless and needy see me as possibly having value, apparently in the form of spare change and cigarettes, and call out to me. The two occupy separate worlds with some overlapping parts that force them to share a few places, like the DMV or the courtroom. I belong to neither one world nor the other and each one thinks I come from the other. I have either become invisible to half the people or half invisible to all of the people, like a ghost. Yet I am greeted by the homeless, hey brother, and unacknowledged by the economically viable. Do I, then, fit in with the homeless? Do they feel invisible too? Do I fit in with the other who pretend to be invisible when it suits them? Or do I truly fit in with neither?

I can see a five story apartment building ahead to the right. The apartments, like many things in Lowell, are in a converted manufacturing building. Straight ahead and passing behind that, is an even bigger five story apartment conversion that has the Historical Society offices in the basement, complete with gift shops, art galleries and memorial displays in honor of Jack Karouac, a fine celebrated example of drunken self-indulgence. With the residents and the history buffs everywhere, it can be busy here. It isn't so busy that I am unable hide from certain viewing angles for a short time. If the need to pee becomes acute enough, I will take my chances on being seen while attempting to hide. The economically viable would probably be able to see me pretty well if I was pissing in the middle of their Historical Society parking lot. When it finally is acute enough and I decide on a place to go, I wonder about the spot. If it is isolated enough for someone to stand there and piss during the middle of the afternoon, is it a good spot in which to lie down for a night or shoot up and nod off? I can see no evidence that anyone has been here, but other than needles and feces, I don't know what to look for. No one would be here now because it is hot, still and sticky off the little corner of the large lot. What if someone were walking around, looking for a place to sleep, though? This is protected a little by the post end of a fence with a bush on the other side and single tree. Granted, the fence isn't much protection because it is chain-link, but it's better than nothing. I have seen plenty of guys sleeping on the unprotected benches around the town, so protection probably doesn't matter. Could this be an undesirable isolated spot? Is there such a thing? Maybe it's too close to people. There is no room for a tent here, there is barely room to get out of the lot and I constantly look around as I urinate. Maybe the vagrants need a bigger place, big enough to make a camping area or a tent city like I have heard is somewhere down on the canal. I am able to get it done and leave the area without being seen. Well, at least without being approached and called to task. Maybe I should be proud that I can learn from past mistakes. Another proud moment in my list of successes, or formative experiences, I suppose.

I had gone to a party at a Hilton with my girlfriend, Alicia. We had dated for a while, long enough for me to have met her parents, but that didn't mean we were married. I was a proud adherent of the playboy lifestyle, though I didn't exactly say I was a playboy. I more sort of implied it. I didn't feel I had to hide it; it was well known that I was irresistible to women and Alicia accepted it because she understood my magnetism. The truth is, though, that I didn't tell Alicia anything at all about my playboy lifestyle. I want to say that I assumed she knew about it and accepted it because she cared so much about me. The truth is that I hid it from her. Some friends of hers had rented rooms on the 6th floor. We met them at room 622 or 632 or 692 or something like that. It doesn't matter now and it didn't then. What did matter was that I knew of only one room and there were about 25 people in it, including some pretty attractive girls. After we were there for a while, I think some tension developed in the room. Alicia didn't say anything, but I am relatively sure that she, along with some of her friends, did not approve of the way I behaved towards Betsy or Bessy or something like that. She was not one of Alicia's friends. Bevvy and I were getting along just great, I thought. She was nice and friendly when we met and began talking. We drank our wine or coolers or beers and she giggled at some of my jokes or showed great interest in some of my opinions. I figured that she was pretty into me as I was so funny and so smart. It seems possible now that she was actually just being polite. As time passed, she may have become less friendly as I became more so. As the booze went down on top of the beer or the other way around, who remembers, and Betsy disappeared, I began to feel some discomfort in my stomach. Alicia had also disappeared, but there were plenty of eyes on me, mostly sideways glances. With all that I had ingested, I couldn't navigate very well. I couldn't reason very well either, but I did know that something had to be done. The discomfort was not due to the tension I had created but due to the fact that I had to take a crap and soon. I looked around for a place to go. Happily, there are bathrooms at the Hilton. Unhappily, the bathrooms are rooms situated within the socializing rooms and the one I was in was full of people. I was too befuddled to go in search of other rooms much less a bathroom in the lobby or somewhere and I had lost all of my support when I lost track of Alicia. There weren't many options for me. When I went into the bathroom, everyone predictably vanished from it. Being disliked has advantages.

I locked the door and sat on the toilet, sloppily timing myself because I was in a hurry. I figured on a quick release, in and out, do the business and get out before anybody knows what happened. Right. I had made a miscalculation and could not have been more mistaken. I did not make a quick deposit and escape or even have a normal bowel movement. I had some kind of an episode, an intestinal cleansing that made me feel a little fortunate to have that awful pile out of me. My time was way off and people were trying to spread from room number one into room number two, the bathroom. Having a bathroom does not ensure that there is toilet paper in it. It is not surprising given the length of time and the number of people, especially girls, at the party using the toilet paper. There weren't even any tissues. I took the only thing available in the room and wet down a bulky Hilton towel to wipe my soiled backside. It sounds simple, but it's easier said than done and afterward, what could I do with the ruined linen? Again, the options were limited. Instead of the sink, the floor, or the tiny trashcan next to the door, I chose the bathtub because I could pull the curtain to hide the shitty towel and the hand towel I had to use as a hygiene supplement. At least the toilet didn't clog. That was probably because there was no paper in it.

I was hoping against hope that everyone except maybe a couple of guys had left during my long stay in the bathroom. When I finally opened the door, it was to find a group waiting to use the little room which I had fouled so horribly. There were some guys, sure, but also several very pretty young ladies, including my own lovely Alicia. I could only have felt more shame if I were less drunk. I remember saying something about there being no paper in there as the group looked at me with strange expressions, anger and disgust, and I edged toward the entry door. Alicia was slowly shaking her head as she stared at me. It was easy enough to escape the room as palpable animosity seemed to squeeze me toward the door. The memory is more difficult to escape and I wish it had happened to someone else. But I know it was me.

So much for being in control of things. I want to blame the whole thing on my impairment, but how would that exonerate me? Nobody did any of it to me or forced me to do anything. Some of them may even have wanted to force me to stop. I brought the impairment on myself and acted poorly on my own. It was my own lack of judgment, lack of discipline and control that led to that episode. How, then, can I trust my own judgments or opinions? It might be a good strategy to ask the opinion of others about some things. I bet that if I asked Alicia for an opinion at some point that night, she would have given me something useful, like her opinion that I stop drinking. If I had asked anyone else his or her opinion, any one of them may have given me something good, like leave Becky alone. Some people, though, consider that a cop out. I have heard someone say to just be yourself, but what if yourself is someone that everyone hates? I think it's possible that each of us is one person in one circumstance and another person in a different circumstance, but each of us can choose some behaviors to follow and remain fairly constant. If we are unsure of a behavior, we can ask someone. We don't have to follow the advice, but at least there are options and it might help. The only expectations held by the people at that party were that everyone act in a mildly friendly manner. They assumed that everyone was sharing something: an event, a story, social interaction, bonding. But I didn't ask anything of any of them, not even my partner Alicia; I was just being myself. In acting in such a socially perverse way, I had violated the agreement I made with these people by attending their party. Which one of them wanted me to be myself? Which version of myself did any of them want? Whichever version any of them wanted, it was not the one any of them got. I have heard that each of us is only the sum of our deeds, but I sure hope that's not true. If we are the sum of our deeds, I hope that some are weighed more heavily than others. I wonder which weighs more, making a spectacular ruin of the bathroom at the giant party or spurning the social contract. If there are different versions of myself, it's going to take some contemplation to figure out who is making agreements for me. It will take even more contemplation to figure out what agreements were made, especially in my latest calamity. I would like to figure out what ones I violated that pushed me to the place I currently occupy. I don't have the energy for that. Instead, I have been working lately on making no agreements.

As I leave my makeshift urinal, I look around to

see if there is anyone in the area who might have observed me. I don't see anybody and I walk up the paved slope through the lot toward the river on the other side of DTL. When I first heard of DTL it confused me. I didn't admit that because I didn't want to look stupid. Who wouldn't know where DTL is? After looking at those kiosk maps posted on many of the streets and walking all over looking, I finally broke down and asked someone, my fictitious girlfriend Katrina. I probably could have asked one of the geniuses at her bar, but I didn't want to make any more friends. If I set a precedent by talking to one of those guys, who knew where it would end? I didn't need a best buddy. So I might look stupid to Katrina, but I didn't think she would break up with me for it because I over-tip. I didn't need to worry about making another friend. She did ask one of the intellectuals present to tell me and I was informed that DTL is Down Town Lowell, obviously. It made sense after I heard it, but what's so obvious about it? I've never heard anyone say DTB when referring to Downtown Boston or DTN for Downtown Nashua. That's one more thing I know about the city that I didn't know before. It probably came about through texting or something so it will be handy knowledge if anyone ever texts me.

CHAPTER NINE

Even though we seem made for each other, seem to belong together, there are a lot of things I don't know about this place. I don't know all of the laws or rules. I'm sure the city has a standard set of laws like everywhere else and some ordinances specific to this city. Is urinating outside here OK, is it a violation of a social convention, or is it illegal? If relieving oneself outdoors in the city is not illegal, it seems wrong and I don't want anyone to see me do it. I would like to be able to say that I have too much modesty and class. I would also like to say it's too private to share with others. Really, though, I just want to stay out of sight. There is a reason people don't go to the bathroom wherever they want. You don't see a guy standing on the sidewalk in front of Finn's Pub pissing, or standing outside of the Registry of Motor Vehicles or Subway or the book store. It could be that enough people relieved themselves outside that something had to be done; a law had to be created. If it is illegal, I don't want to get caught. Lowell has no shortage of policemen to enforce the law. Unless you ask the mayor, that is, who claims to need more police officers and so needs more funding. Maybe he needs more laws to support more policemen and pissing outdoors is one of them. I wonder how those fools with the dirty ball caps outside of Katrina's would handle it. Maybe one of them was the mayor. There is always the danger of being arrested no matter what you do and I don't want to be arrested. I said that after the first time.

I had met Helen while registering during orientation for one of my attempts at school. She was helpful, vivacious and exotically pretty. She should have been wearing a grass skirt and a lei. It turned out that we had the same interests, namely keg parties, cookouts and philosophical discussions. I got to know her boyfriend too and he was OK, though we were never really that close. We all got along pretty well and hung around in the same circles, though her boyfriend had other interests and he was around less frequently. She listened to everything I said with great attention, like I was some kind of wise man or something. Boy, was that good for the confidence. The more she hung on my every word, the closer I grew to her and the more we hung around. She was smart, energetic and organized, organized enough that she was able to conduct two relationships without any difficulty. Well, maybe a little difficulty but I wasn't worried about it. It was still quite a trick since we did things, fun things. We went to ball games because I liked them, museum displays because she liked them, day trips to the beach, weekends at a random festival, even a weekend here and there as a couple on some activity trip, like canoeing or sightseeing. She was able to somehow organize all of this simultaneously with two relationships, one with her boyfriend and one with me. And she found me so fascinating that my vanity would not be denied.

After a while, her boyfriend got kind of shut out even though he remained her boyfriend. He seemed fairly fine with everything, as if he didn't care or didn't know. He would still socialize with everyone, but I was a little distant with him and Helen seemed that way too, but maybe that was only when I was around. She would tell me that he made little mean comments to her here and there. It seemed to me that she trying to make me protective, like I would take her and comfort her and protect her from mean comments. It didn't work. I was dubious about the comments because I thought it uncharacteristic of him, but who knows how a guy will act when his feelings are hurt or if he is suspicious? Were his feelings hurt? He never showed any signs of it. Was he suspicious? He never showed signs of that either, but how was it possible that he not know what was going on with Helen and me? It seemed pretty obvious to me. Did he know about it but overlook it? I guess I can understand that, maybe, if he was waiting for her to finish a fling before they settled down to a faithful life of contentment. I thought petty cruelties by him seemed unlikely in light of the fact that they stayed together. I also had doubts about the quality of the discourse which she found so fascinating, mine. Because I didn't completely trust her, I didn't completely want her as my own girlfriend. I guess she trusted me because she often pushed for a more serious relationship. If I did become her partner, what would she do without my knowledge? How would I know if she was being my partner or if she was being, well, my Helen?

I began to spend some nights off campus at Helen's. My place was in a separate male dormitory along with most of the other guys. If we got too loaded at one of our events, though, I would sneak her into my dormitory. After one sweaty concert or beer pong match or softball game, I decided to shower after I snuck our sweaty bodies into the dorm. With only a little bit of coercion, Helen joined me for purposes of mutual cleanliness. We washed and laughed and screeched, she screeched, not me, until someone called us out of the shower. It could have been all of the noise that attracted the police. Who would call the police? I knew all of the guys in that dorm and none of them would be disturbed by the happy racket from the men's shower in the wee hours. There were two policemen and a dog. That explained it. They were doing a random drug search walk-through. It must have been slow in the war on drugs and I guess they were bored that night. I didn't think they would do it but, sure enough, they ran us into the police station. When they got us there, I felt pretty sorry for myself and horribly guilty for Helen's sake. Those hard-asses couldn't put themselves in our position and just stop us or lecture us or anything. Maybe it was the screeching that turned them into soldiers of virtue wielding the sword of justice. Or maybe they were just cops. There were maybe a half dozen other cops at the station and the population of our community was not large enough for this incident to remain a secret, especially since it was sure to appear in the police activity section of the community paper. I tried to take the blame and keep Helen from being charged with something, but the cops weren't having it. I wondered how this would affect her relationship with her boyfriend. The incident did make the paper in the police blog and some of our friends did read about it. That was a relationship that I controlled until the end. When she and I stopped seeing each other quite a while later, it was unrelated to her arrest. When she and her boyfriend became unattached some time later than that, it was also unrelated to her arrest.

I wondered what Helen told her boyfriend to keep their relationship alive for as long it was. Did she lie to him, or tell him the truth as she saw it, a truth that he could accept? Did she tell him nothing? The truth. I've heard that the truth hurts. In that case, who wants it?

I've also heard that if five people witness the same thing, there will be five different versions of the truth. If the truth is that she slept around, it seems that there would be a different version that would make it OK to anyone who heard it. I bet her explanation of the illegal incident leading to our arrest was different from mine. I bet that any of the many people who knew what was going on over the course of those long happy months would have a different description of our relationship than either Helen's or mine. So what is the truth? The truth all depends on who tells it. If it all depends upon who is telling it, doesn't that make it an opinion? Is it possible that there is no such thing as the truth? She probably didn't leave a lot of incriminating clues around, but I figured our thing was obvious anyway. Whether her boyfriend was blind from wishful thinking or had his eyes closed out of weakness, it makes no difference. What kind of a jackass could have such blindness to obfuscation, dissimulation and infidelity? Maybe he had his own version of the truth. My opinion of Helen's boyfriend is very low and always will be, though he was a nice enough guy. She gets a lot of my respect, though, for being able to pull it off. Or, unless, maybe, had he known everything all along? Is it possible, maybe he just loved her?

Hard questions sometimes force themselves on me. I wonder what anyone wants when he or she asks for the truth. I think probably he wants to hear what he hopes, not what's true. Does it tell anything about him if he never asks for the truth? Maybe he doesn't want to know the answer. Does he even want honesty from someone he only likes, never mind someone he loves? Was Helen being honest when she was so interested in my blather? Do I want to know everything that made Lucy who she was? I think Lucy knew more about me than she let on. Did I underestimate the depth of her love? On the other hand, I don't think I ever got the whole truth from Rebecca, and I was devoted to her. Did I overestimate the depth of her love? What would have been different if I had known everything about her? Did I keep my eyes closed during that crippling last disaster? There's this feeling I have that I don't like. Not one bit. It's the feeling that I already know the answer.

CHAPTER TEN

When I called her after so much time in that beach chair on a hardwood floor, she didn't answer the phone. The recorded message informed me that Rebecca was unavailable to pick up the phone at that moment, but she would get back to me as soon as possible. I have to admit that getting the message got me down a little. Though it sounds normal and OK that she couldn't answer the phone, and it may even have been true, I knew she kept her cell phone with her the way an emphysema sufferer keeps her inhaler, and she used to answer her phone anywhere. I guess she wasn't as focused on her phone as I was on mine. Worse, I had not prepared to leave a message. I left a stumbling hello and call me back message. We had not spoken in so long that any eloquence I had or residual confidence that remained had oozed into a deep black hole of clutching need. When she called back after a while, she sounded almost as tentative as me. I wonder if she was hiding irritation or consternation at having to make that call. Did she see the number when I called, look at the ceiling and say, Ah Shit, then get her thoughts together and call me back? I remember where I was when I made and then received the first call: I sat on a swing next to the baseball park. It was early afternoon on a still and sunny day, muggy and hot. I didn't know it then, or for a long long time, but today that is the place and time that I identify as the end. That is the spot where we had the first conversation of our afterlife. It wasn't much of a conversation as far as they go, but it was the first. It didn't fix anything or change anything or even enlighten me on anything, but it did end the silence. I walked back down the block to the apartment and sat with my phone.

I feel kind of like the guy in a movie that I saw once who gets stranded on an island for a few years. When he gets rescued and returns to civilization, everyone has forgotten him and moved on. His wife has remarried, his children have grown and have families of their own, his dog has gone to a better world and all of his friends have become strangers. If he had made a big issue of it, if he had staked his claim as an important figure who deserved their time and attention, I bet he could have inserted himself back into the lives of his former wife, children and friends. After all, none of it was his fault. He was very gracious about it, though. He didn't make a big fuss or anything; he just left town and let everybody live their lives. Heroic. That is in the movies. Somehow, I thought that I would be like the guy in a book, the first book. When Odysseus returned to his home after being lost at sea for twenty years, his wife had held out against suitors and waited for him out of loyalty and love for all of that time. His dog, loyal and loving until his return, waited for him before giving in to old age and dying at Odysseus's feet. His son, too, grew to manhood while loyally awaiting his return. All of his colleagues and acquaintances, though, had spent all of those years partying at his house, eating his food and hitting on his wife. They got theirs, though. When Odysseus figured out what was going on, he hacked them to pieces with a sword or pierced them through with arrows and he butchered them all. Heroic. In real life, I am mostly like the guy who is told to go away, he slinks away quietly, wanders around and gets lost, then disappears, is forgotten and never says anything about it. Pathetic. I don't know the book or the movie of that story.

CHAPTER ELEVEN

I stop on a pedestrian bridge over the canal and look at the dark water barely moving. It's not flowing right now because of those tour boats that are on the canals. I can see the light granite of the canal's side near the surface edge, so I know the water isn't black. It's just dirty. It looks kind of far down to the water from here, but it isn't as far as it looks. If I were going to commit suicide, I couldn't do it if I were to throw myself in here. It's only about ten feet to the styrofoam, paper, plastic and a shoe? trapped in the film on the surface of the water. The biggest deterrent to suicide isn't the debris but the possibility of botching it, I think. It might work if I landed on something sharp that someone has thrown into the canal like a shower rod or one of those floor to ceiling lamps. It would have to go through my eye or maybe my heart, though. I think it's too much of a long shot. Plus, it would probably hurt a lot. I won't do it. I would probably get stuck through the bladder or bowels and have to wear a colostomy bag. More likely the fungus from the discarded cups or syringes in the dirty water would give me some bacteria that would eat away my intestines and force me to wear a colostomy bag. What if I were to go to a bigger bridge, one of those over the Merrimack, and throw myself off? I don't like that idea either. It doesn't look as high from a little distance as it does from the bridge itself. There are rocks in there that could probably do the trick. But what if I just hit my head and got brain damage? What if I broke my back? What if I did both? Jumping off a bridge doesn't sound very good. Life could be worse.

Shooting myself doesn't sound like a very good way to commit suicide either. It seems too violent and loud, like I would be assaulting myself. Plus, it would have to be a good shot and I think only the head or the heart would work. If I tried a shot to the head and botched it, I might only give myself brain damage and possibly a colostomy bag. Or I could just shoot out an eye or an ear. Or maybe both like my cousin Cecil. He didn't do it himself, but he did get shot in the head. He wasn't even attempting suicide. Somebody else shot him in the face when he was trying to assault some woman. It went in next to his left eye and went out behind his right ear. He didn't die from it either, but he did lose sight in his left eye and hearing in his right ear. He did commit suicide in a way. He drank so much booze and took so many drugs that he died many years later from liver or kidney complications. Even his long stints in prison for assaulting women, where he couldn't have any drugs or booze, didn't get his organs cleaned up enough to save him. One guy I knew a long time ago actually did shoot himself in a suicide attempt. Presumably, he went for the heart and he botched it. He missed his heart by a mile. He shot himself in the abdomen with a rifle and he didn't die from his gunshot either. After crawling on his hands and knees through the yard from his garage, where the gun was, to his kitchen, where the phone was, he called an ambulance for himself. He followed up his dramatic suicide attempt with counseling. What a letdown. So much for the tragic/romantic finale.

It seems the popular modern way to go is pills, but I don't know about that. All it takes is to swallow a few pills, drink a bunch of liquor, take a nap and check out.

Easy peasy. It sounds pretty simple but too many times I have heard about someone surviving it. Too many times the person is found unconscious, brought to the hospital for a stomach pump, survives and is branded as a person who cried out for help. A crybaby. There is also the possibility of failing and just being fucked up forever, with slow speech and slow eyes as if always half drunk, and a colostomy bag. Suicide by police is not an attractive option, nor is a suicide bomb. Why make a bunch of enemies on the way out or take a bunch of other people with me? Some of them might be nice. Dousing myself with gasoline and lighting myself on fire? No way. One method that sounds good and actually takes a lot of lives is driving really fast and smashing into something. It's better than lighting myself on fire, but not very reliable.

CHAPTER TWELVE

I went to the Halloween party by myself. Well, when I met a bunch of people I wasn't by myself, but I attended unaccompanied. I kind of like the idea of Halloween, though the way everybody acts these days makes it less eerie and mysterious than it should be. It is observed in such an overblown manner that it isn't eerie or mysterious at all. It is a parody of what Halloween is supposed to signify; that the barriers are down between the living and the dead. It's a night when we are all supposed to be closest to the other side. Ghosts walk among the living checking to see how close we are to the joining them, ready to whisk someone away who gets too close to the world of the dead. Tombstones and graveyards appear on the lawns of some people and ghosts of all sizes are everywhere. It seems like Halloween would be the night to be most careful. Everyone knows that the ghosts are among us, with the possible exception of Jehovah's Witnesses. They don't believe in Halloween. Many Halloweens before the last one I celebrated, my last one with her, a Jehovah's Witness in our town did not pass out candy to the children who went to his door. That would have been fine, except this non-believer had a carved pumpkin perched on the body of a stuffed suit sitting in a chair on his front steps. He had fake spiders and webs decorating his windows, a witch silhouette on the front door and candles in the windows. His house was decorated pretty elaborately for someone who didn't observe the event. When children were drawn to his house, assuming he adhered to Halloween tradition, he refused to pass out anything because he said he didn't believe in Halloween.

When I returned home from the party at or near the witching hour and I learned about this neighbor's hypocrisy, I decided to set things right. I was going to do that for all of the children, naturally. I found as many eggs as I could because tossing eggs at the house is the traditional response in this situation. I also took every other discarded piece of food I could find which included a chicken carcass, baked potatoes, carrots and a half a carton of spoiled milk. I grabbed my brother as co-pilot and we headed out to set the world right. Except for the nasty stench in the car everything went great at first. I cruised by the house and observed no lights or movement. I cruised by again, slowly, shut off the lights, stopped the car and we pelted that house with everything we had taken from the discarded food pile. Though dark, we could still make out egg splatter on a front window next to the front door and vegetable debris on the front steps. Beside the scarecrow in the chair was a gnawed chicken carcass that came to rest after bouncing off the front storm door in front of the witch, and a milk carton rested on the lawn. Bub and I hopped into the car and I raced us off.

It was pretty gratifying for a few minutes. I wasn't completely satisfied with our work, though. I felt that we were missing something or had forgotten something. I drove by the house again and was disappointed that I couldn't tell that there was a chicken carcass on the steps and eggs on the window. I could tell, however, that there was a big scarecrow with a pumpkin for a head sitting in a chair on the front steps. I figured that was what we missed and it would make us feel better if we got that scarecrow. My co-pilot wasn't really enthusiastic, but he finally agreed that having the Halloween decorations out was insulting if you didn't even observe Halloween. It's kind of like a Hindu with a dot on his forehead wearing a big cross into the Catholic Church in order to drink all of the wine. On the next pass by the house, I shut off the lights as we approached, stopped the car in front of the house, we jumped out and grabbed the stuffed scarecrow and his pumpkin head from the front steps. We even took the chair, wrestled all of it into the back of the car, jumped in and raced off. As we discussed what to do with the scarecrow, we drove by the town library at the intersection of two streets and suddenly hit upon the brilliant idea of placing the chair, scarecrow and pumpkin on the roof of the town library. That way, everyone could see it and appreciate the fact that betrayers of the Halloween spirit had been humbled. Getting the things up there wasn't easy, but I was helped by the spirits around that night and my co-pilot. Using the uneven stones of the wall as a ladder, I scaled the two-story flagstone structure in the back where it was dark so that no passing cars could see me. Bub managed to pass me the things so that I could situate them perfectly on the peak of the roof facing the parking lot and the road. I was pleased when I climbed down and saw that it worked out just as we had hoped. The scarecrow looked almost lifelike sitting proudly in the chair illuminated by a street light as if observing traffic through the dark holes it had for eyes. Jehovah's Witnesses make really good Halloween decorations.

My mind was probably heightened with our success or maybe from the earlier celebrating, and I was inspired. Maybe with that little success came hubris. I couldn't resist taking us back by the house to view our work. Although Bub was against it, I couldn't be deterred, and I was driving. As I slowed the car and turned off my lights, the SUV parked next to the house turned on his lights. That Jehovah's Witness was waiting in his vehicle. I guess they don't believe in turning the other cheek, either. I hit the gas and turned on the lights, speeding away from the pursuing Bronco. Our car was faster, by a lot. The road I took was pretty straight for a while before it became curvy. When I hit the second curve, the momentum from the first curve was too much for the bulky car and it would not, it could not, stay on the road. I hurled the car into the embankment on the road shoulder which acted as a catapult, shooting us into the air. I reached over and grabbed my passenger, pulling him toward me across the bench seat of the big old car. For what? Maybe I wanted to have him near as we set off into the unknown. Maybe it was an attempt to assuage my own fear. Maybe it was just the reaction to grab at the closest living thing at the moment that the fabric of reality exploded into brilliant screeching light. Maybe I didn't want to go alone into the incomprehensible howl of angels or ghosts or God as we careened through everything in the world. I had a sense of wonder as the transformer exploded above our faces in the windshield, engulfing and showering the car with hissing vivid pieces of the night sky. I had flown us through blackness and demolished the moon. The pieces flared and pulsated around us as they dropped by the windows in irregular sizes. We were in a meteor shower in space and the meteors were phosphorescent orbs of beauty. We did stop, though, after the car finished smashing through small trees, big branches and sheered a telephone pole off at 15 feet. We came to rest in a little clearing of smashed and destroyed saplings about four feet from the ground, surrounded by broken limbs, pine boughs and wires from the telephone pole I had splintered. I snapped out of awe as the car was crackling and steaming and I thought fire, explosion, destruction, police and I said to Bub, let's go! It took me a couple of tries to get him to answer me. Finally, he did answer saying that he didn't think he could go. He was hurt somehow.

Later I learned that I had knocked out the power in the area. I had also knocked out Bub and broken his collar bone. The police, fire fighters, EMTs and the bystanders who materialized from the dark all said how lucky we were to have survived. I didn't feel so lucky, but I was. I was lucky I didn't kill my brother. The passenger's side of the car was crushed. If I had not grabbed his jacket in terror and pulled him toward me over the bench seat of the old car, he also would have been crushed and who knows how many parts of him I would have broken. I think that attempting anything in a speeding automobile is a bad idea. Crashing one is certain only to mutilate something or someone and death is determined by luck of the draw. It's a good method only for unintentionally destroying things that you love. Unless a guy wants to make his unbearable life even more miserable, suicide in a car is the wrong way to go. I would say, I have said, that I pulled my brother across the seat thereby saving him from being mangled by the tree I partially put us into. I would imply that I saved his life by acting quickly and heroically and I single handedly turned certain tragedy into a wild adventure. But I know that it's what I want other people to believe. I would like to believe it myself, but I don't. It's not true. I wasn't trying to commit suicide, but I came close to dying from regret that Halloween. Hurting Bub like that put a laceration in my spirit that I didn't know was there at first. It healed poorly and now I can feel it like scar tissue from an old whip wound across my back.

After saving my brother's life, I began to understand in a vague way what I almost did to us. The concept of loving and losing someone began to develop some place in my mind. I started to think or feel in some nebulous manner the strange and unpredictable nature of caring for or loving others. There was no telling where the attachment came from and there still isn't. It has never been a choice I made. The rarity of that treasure wasn't easy to understand then and it's no easier now. I guess I began then to feel lucky to love my family. We grew up together and had known each other for our whole lives, but I didn't choose to love any of them. Nobody is forced to love his or her sibling. What would it be like to live in the house with Cain and Abel, or King Lear's sons Edmund and Edgar? Of all the people that I know and of whom I am fond, those who I actually love are limited. It seems like it's an exclusive group and I picked the best people, like an all-star team. But that isn't true. Even with the limited number of people I love, I haven't picked any of them. Each is unique and each is the most precious thing that I can imagine, but I didn't pick him or her. I don't get to choose the ones I love; love comes around inconspicuously like bad air and infuses me, the next thing I know, I'm in love. Love comes and gets me like it has picked me to go on stage at a hypnotists show. I am probably not alone in that the object of my love doesn't usually have anything to say about it. Until I get to know her.

Now that my arrogance has been sheered away, shredded and reformed into disappointment, I don't want to make a big scene or perpetrate careless destruction. Instead of going about it with a reckless arrogance that is sure to demolish entirely the wrong thing, the surest and most dignified suicide must be the classic method practiced by disgraced Roman aristocrats. I could sit in a hot tub, slice my wrists and bleed to death quietly and comfortably. It is also the simplest. I have a knife, I have a tub and that's all I need. The hot water apparently causes the veins to dilate and the heart to pump faster than sitting someplace cold. That sounds better than what disgraced Japanese aristocrats practiced. They would stab themselves in the stomach with a sword and cut across the abdomen, disemboweling themselves. I think I would rather shoot myself. I guess I won't kill myself today. Besides, how dignified would it be to slit my wrists in the little bathroom of my little apartment? The second biggest deterrent to committing suicide is losing dignity. I don't have to commit suicide right this moment, anyway. There will be plenty of time for that, for as long as I live.

CHAPTER THIRTEEN

I leave the pedestrian bridge over the canal to walk toward the river and find myself face to face with a train. It's a stationary locomotive, coal car, and passenger car resting on a track embedded in the sidewalk, so it isn't going to run me down. That's good because I don't want to go out like that. The train is neat and clean as if it has recently been painted or washed. Boston and Maine is stenciled on the side, like the train is giving everyone a message. It says, if you wonder what I am and what I do, here it is. I am the Boston and Maine line. Or at least I was. It doesn't say why it's in Lowell with me. Also painted on both sides is another message from the train. It says, Keep Off. I like it better. Presumably it ran from Boston to somewhere in Maine, maybe Portland. It looks sturdy and still, like it is being held in suspended animation. If someone were to really restore it, resuscitate it, the locomotive looks like it could still do its job. It is an image of power and accomplishment. I imagine it running on its rails with a steady smoking strength, carrying people and merchandise from Boston to Portland. It would return, huffing and gasping with determined effort, carrying people and raw material from Portland back to Boston. The arms that link the wheels pumping as rain and mist and snow drop on it trying to wet it and coat it but evaporate with the heat created by its effort. The snow would coat the passenger car but melt and drip from the locomotive as it muscles the other cars back to the station and safety. It was a powerhouse, a force to be admired. The things it could carry over the distance it travelled a feat that very few could accomplish. I wonder where it went, how fast it could go, how much coal it used, who and how many people it carried each way. I also wonder why it's in Lowell. Did the train lose its purpose and drift around for a while, wondering what went wrong and doing little or nothing to help itself find another purpose? It drifted along until it found itself stuck in the street in Lowell, motionless, powerless; its spirit drained, evaporated. I could find out what happened easily enough since the National Streetcar Museum is right across the pedestrian bridge. But that would be too much trouble. I would have to make a commitment. Maybe I will do it another day, not today. It's not a real train now, anyway, even though it was once. Now it's just a monument, a relic found, restored and given a new life by the city. It's not much of a life, really. It just sits there and looks good, of no use to anyone any longer. It was replaced by something. Maybe it was trucks.

Did someone come along and woo the manufacturing companies away from the railroad? Did the companies begin to look at the trucks with some interest when a guy came along to sweet talk them and the truck guy persuaded them to try the trucks because they were new and different? Just try them once with no strings attached and see how good it would be. The manufacturing company tried it once and liked it. And then again. And again. After the companies had the trucks on the side a few times, they decided to try them for a while and see. Did the truck guy convince the companies that the trucks would be a better fit for them than the train? The trucks would keep them satisfied; the trucks had more panache. He would say that trucks are more graceful, more modern, could get in places that the train can't. The trucks would be a much better partner for the companies. The trucks would make the companies happy. The reliability and power and might of the train became undesirable. Its steady work ethic and commitment became boring. Eventually, the companies stopped using the unexciting, well-known train to use the new, more accommodating trucks. What did the train do wrong? Nothing. It was just being itself, being a train. And the trucks, well, the trucks actually were more exciting. Did the manufacturing companies ever miss the train? The companies aren't even around anymore, but the trucks are. They are hooked up with other manufacturers. And here is the train. In the end, was the replacement better or just different?

Patricia and I were in bed asleep at our apartment near the beach on the night our relationship changed, although in truth it had probably changed already without our acknowledgment. It had remained in stasis for as long as earthly possible. We had lived together for a while and it had worked out pretty well; she had needed a roommate and a lover, I had needed a room and a lover. Beautiful, wise and sophisticated, she was everything I could want in a roommate and lover. Energetic, fit and eager, I was everything she wanted, too. One morning we had gone snorkeling in a nearby cove followed by a picnic together on the adjacent glade overlooking the water. I was pretty impressed with it all and I didn't think life could get any better. When she broached the subject of becoming roommates, I thought life just got better. It would be just me and her, and her two year old daughter from her second marriage. I didn't worry about how it would work out. That was a detail that was beyond me. Since it would be the off-season, the little beach resort would be kind of dead, so we would have it nearly all to ourselves and we could stroll around together without crowds jostling us. She had a good stroll, I thought, sort of haughty. When we had first met, she lived in a dump in the projects. After some party or other she started a wrestling match with me, which I lost, but then I won. At that time, she was looking for a lover and I was one. I didn't know why she chose me, but I was all for it.

Maybe it was the way I looked working the fryolator behind the food pickup shelves in the restaurant. She was a waitress when I began working. With my sweaty face and grease spattered apron, I must have caught her eye. After work sometimes, the restaurant gang would get together and socialize. Maybe it was my social skill that attracted her. We would gather where we were or we would go to someone's apartment to drink and vent and share work stories. If we were having a good enough time, the night would often become morning. They were friendly gatherings where we all bonded over our shared experience and built camaraderie among the group. After a while, Patricia showed more interest in me and apparently everyone was not thrilled with that. At someone's apartment during one of our gatherings, one of our group wanted an activity to entertain himself and, I suppose, everyone else. He wanted to have a friendly slap contest in which he and another participant would trade friendly slaps. The two of them would stand at arm's length and each would reach out to gently cuff the face of the other. Each was supposed to move his head away quickly enough to avoid being hit and whoever delivered the most slaps wins. It sounded like fine entertainment, for somebody else. He didn't want to play with somebody else; he wanted to play with me. I declined again and again until it became a little embarrassing. He could juggle pretty well, why didn't he do that? I had seen him juggle knives in the restaurant kitchen before and it was sort of impressive. He didn't want to juggle; he wanted to friendly slap fight with me.

When I finally agreed in spite of my reluctance, the host sent us outside for the game because he didn't want any violence in his home. With everyone watching out the window, it was a fun little diversion full of happiness and festivity until Joel slapped me across the face a couple of times. The contest didn't feel that friendly and the slaps didn't feel that gentle. I thought I perceived a malicious pleasure in his eyes and a slight smirk on his mouth as he slapped my face again for his audience. It may have been his pleasure that annoyed me; then again, it may have been the slaps across my face. I grabbed his shoulder and arm, swung him in a semicircular arc and slammed his body into the fender and bumper of a car. I bet our host was glad he had sent us outside. If we were in the apartment, that definitely would have broken an end table or a lamp. When he started to rise from his side, I slapped his face hard enough to knock him back down. I straddled him and slapped his face five times, once for each time he had slapped mine and once for good measure. I got an extra one in because when I slapped him to the ground I didn't count that one. When we got back to the party, he got a little sympathy because his hands were bloody where I had ground them into the parking lot with my knees. After that, Joel didn't ask me to slap fight any more. Maybe Patricia saw a weakness in my game. Just a few hours after that, she beat me in a wrestling match.

We walked the beach, strolled among the closed shops, and held hands over the ocean crags. We went to the work parties, went to family things and stayed inside bundled up. We listened to Joni Mitchel and Cat Stevens and I marveled at the discovery. Our time was sometimes idyllic even though many of our days were spent doing child things for the little girl. But that has a reward of its own and it was good. There was something fulfilling in doing nice things for someone who only wants kindness. We would go with her to the park or take her to day-care at her grandmother's. We all did fun things together and I thought she was sweet little girl. We got along well and I was fond of her, which was a good thing because I ended up spending a lot more time with the little girl than I would have thought had I known more about life. The longer we were together the more nights and sometimes days Patricia began spending out doing stuff with friends or with her former mother in law. She also spent at least a week every other month in New Jersey or someplace visiting her brother. Usually, I spent the time with her daughter, making sure she ate and got to her grandmother's house. If not exactly traditional, it was all very common and proper. As far as I knew, it was the way everyone was.

When were awakened that night by the phone, it was late and I waited for it to stop ringing. I couldn't wait too long, though; there was a baby in the house. Besides, it was so late that it couldn't be a random sales call. It could be one of Patricia's chat buddies. I didn't want to answer it. The caller was my mother. My Dad had gotten into a car accident and had been taken to the hospital. How soon could I make it? Stunned and foggy, I looked for advice. Patricia told me not to go. Don't go. Don't go. You can't go. I told my mother that Patricia said I couldn't go. It was my mother's turn to be stunned and she was anything but foggy. She said she would pick me up. So I had to choose; did I do what my mother said or did I do what Patricia said? Patricia took me to the hospital instead and it was as big an ordeal as she had predicted. The one who should not have gone to the hospital was Patricia.

I think that was the point when our relationship became more work than she was prepared to expend on it. We had reached the end of the perfect fantasy. A sexual fantasy that comes when you see someone you have never met and begin to imagine what it would be like to have him or her; her desire and abandon with you. I had done all of the things I would do with her in my imagination. She had gotten her fantasy more than me, because she had actually had the fantasy and had orchestrated the whole thing while I didn't know I was having it. Her imagination was much more developed than mine was. The fantasy had run its course and real life pushed into my idyll. Questions began to arise that I never would have imagined. Did I use a different towel every time I took a shower? Why? I was creating piles of laundry that she had to do. Was I eating certain foods in the refrigerator that were on her diet? Was I leaving my things strewn around the bedroom? Was I leaving the toilet seat up? I found myself committing a multitude of small infractions that were adding up to a big breach, but I thought I need only correct the little infractions. I didn't recognize the signals to a sizeable fracture, like small pebbles cast a distance away from a mountainside collapse. I was witnessing while participating in something I did not understand. I could have been having a hallucination and I was lying on the bed in the sun with my pants down, vulnerable. I had just had an orgasm and was leaving the envelope of the fantasy.

One day I searched her car for her comb or

necklace or shopping list. Instead, I found pictures of her during the time she was last visiting in New Jersey. She was standing on a beach wearing a happy smile and a one piece bathing suit that made her body look as if it had been carefully sculpted and caressed until any imperfection had been smoothed away or disappeared into the gentle curves accentuated by the suit. Well, half of her body anyway. The other half was not visible because her arms were wrapped around a dark haired guy who had one arm around her waist. He was also wearing a happy smile and a Speedo. Although I had never met her brother, I had seen his picture. And although the pictures of him were from a long time before, the guy wearing the little speedo in these pictures looked nothing at all like the guy in the older pictures. Maybe he had changed a lot. In the background was the white sand, the ocean waves and the Jamaica Good Time Bar. I figured that maybe things were less idyllic than I thought; unless it's idyllic for a live-in girlfriend to sneak to Jamaica for a week with another guy. I was kind of suspicious, but I reserved judgment because there could be a good explanation. She could have explained it away easily by telling me it was her brother or chiropractor or personal trainer, anything really. She could have told me it was my imagination and I would have bought it. Well, anything with the exception of the truth. If she had told me that I was looking at her future husband, I would have been hurt. She didn't even bother, though.

When I tried to understand it then, I only grew confused and depressed. When I try to figure it out now, I think I've got it. Understanding what's happening years after the fact isn't the most helpful time, but it's better than nothing. With Patricia, I was pretty far over my head. Even if she had tried to explain it to me, I did not have the capacity to understand any of it. She didn't really sneak that much and didn't have to. Her only lies were ones of omission. Are those even lies at all? When we met, there was a similar age gap between the little girl and me as there was between me and Patricia. One year before, I was leading my High School basketball team to the playoffs, scoring 25 points and grabbing 12 rebounds a game. In my pregame fantasies, that is. In the real games, I wasn't that dominant. Patricia was embroiled in the traumatic disintegration of her second marriage to a guy who would trade her for drugs or a favor of some kind. She was being shut out of her house with her baby while her husband made some nefarious arrangement involving her and resulting in payment of a debt. What was her view of relationships, I wonder? How did she feel about monogamy? How far did she trust her partner? I think that those were not considerations for her when she thought of me. I was her diversion while she searched for stability. I was her young boy toy, a playmate while she shopped for someone who offered her a real relationship. Looking back, I appreciate the way she conducted her entertainment. Don't older experienced men do the same thing with young naïve girls all the time? With the clarity of time and accumulation of experience, I have decided she regretted that it had to end as much as I did. It had to end, though, so that she could get a life for her child and herself. I believe that she would have continued our thing for longer if it were possible. I flatter myself by thinking that I was perfect in the role in which she cast me and I have often wanted to recreate it. I was not arrogant but always humble and polite. Her friends and former in-laws knew what I was to her and they liked me anyway. I thought that she was so sophisticated that I could only do right things if I did as she wished. I was a curious and attentive lover for her. I never knew her prior relationship with Joel, but I'm sure that he wanted to fill that role. She saw my potential for the position and selected me instead. I think that was the first and last position in which I came so close to realizing my potential. But then, I may be lying to myself again. In the end, without understanding or reason or hope, I ran away from home. My lack of experience so very early led me to missteps that led to failure. I decided that I would be in charge of my relationships in the future. I gained so much experience that so very late I am led to different missteps that lead to failure.

I wonder how much love was involved in that relationship. I had it and keep having it, but it's funny how I keep misunderstanding it. I have not been able to figure out love. I wonder if love is finite or not. Is it finite for some people and limitless for others or is it just a different volume for each like lung capacity? Does it have degrees like decibels? Does it expire after a certain length of time, depending on whether it is acknowledged by the lover or the lovee? It seems like it would be of different strength based upon the lover who gives it, but the lovee who receives it also has a lot of input depending on how much the lovee's behavior encourages or inflames the lover. I wonder if the maximum intensity of love is different for each person and if the love itself determines how much a person can take. Do some people have a mechanism like a wide-angle nozzle that naturally diffuses the really intense love so it gets spread out and doesn't damage anything? Does the really intense love overwhelm some people until they lose strength and independence? Or does it fill some with so much pressure that it ruptures or punctures something in them? If each of us were a vessel that could hold a certain amount of love, would some love be so intense that it would burn a hole in the vessel or even burn it up completely? But none of us are vessels. We are organic beings that change and grow. And what about the effects of growth and change? Does love grow and change or just people? If love does grow, how much time does it take for a tiny bit of love to take root? Once it has begun, will time alone make it grow or does it need to be fed and nurtured? If given enough time, will love finish growing and stop or will it continue to grow like the roots on a willow tree in somebody's back yard that always grow so much that they destroy the water pipes to the home? How can something that keeps growing and changing be understood, much less controlled? If love stops growing but the person continues, will there be a sort of chemical reaction that changes everything? Will love die of boredom or perhaps starve or rot and turn to black disdain? Can someone tell when growing love has reached its peak and will never grow more? If it stops growing short of expectations or of a satisfactory measure, is the lover off the hook for continuing attention to the lovee? Then the lover can withdraw all attention from the former lovee like pulling a table cloth out from under the china on a table prepared for an elegant dinner for two on a terrace in the moonlight. The former lovee will crash to the hard surface of loneliness like wine glasses on the flagstone floor of the terrace. Or is the lover obligated to be kind and let the former lovee down easy as if the former lovee is someone who was cared about and has been unintentionally but unavoidably injured?

CHAPTER FOURTEEN

I get onto the sidewalk behind the train and aim my steps toward the intersection. I walk between the hand-rail protecting the canal and the shrubs that give the path color and life and make it more inviting. The shrubs and rail along the red brick walk-way is a nice disguise that makes walking on the sidewalk a little like walking in a park. Up ahead is a little ramp, stairs and another sitting area with benches next to the street. Those areas are all over the city. They are better than empty pieces of pavement but a bench sitting right next to the street doesn't seem like an inviting place. At least the spot on the canal is quiet, even though it is filled with feces and needles. How relaxing is it to sit on a bench on the street curb while cars sit eight feet away at the red light? I guess you can glare at the drivers as they glare at you while you suck in the exhaust and shake with vibration from the noise of hundreds of cars going through. Those sitting areas are kind of suspicious. What did they replace?

I first met her at a graduation party. At the beginning, there was a house full of people, celebrating, talking, mingling, all very warm and social. The later the hour and the thinner the crowd, the more loose and uninhibited were those remaining. It was during this time of the evening that my eyes were suddenly captured by the unexpected color and carriage of her sweeping through the room and what was left of the crowd. I could see her aura. She was stately yet voluptuous, imperious yet informal. The air wanted to part for her and tried to cling to her at the same time, like me. I was enthralled. I stared and asked who it was. A guy told me not to even think about it. I guess my thoughts showed on my face. I followed her out to the deck, where she was articulately talking at the same time as she was elegantly smoking. I sat listening, wanting to say something insightful on the subject about which I knew nothing. How would she notice me if I sat silently? It turned out that I didn't have to worry about that. She was the girl among the group of us playing truth or dare at the kitchen table after everyone else had left. There had to be a girl. A bunch of guys can't sit around playing truth or dare. There were quite a few dare challenges. I had not played that game before but it seemed like a lot of dares got put out rather than truth answers, like nobody wanted to deal much with the truth. It seemed like we all had a bunch of stuff to hide. I was the second most bold when performing the dare challenges, which may have caught her eye. Rebecca was the boldest. The guy who had told me not to think about her was another player and it turned out they were together. She told me many times in the years to come that they were never committed and the guy was never her boyfriend. He told anybody who would listen to him that she was the love of his life. Though she left with him that night, I was not able to doubt whatever she said. I chose to believe them. He didn't know it, but he had already been replaced.

CHAPTER FIFTEEN

I jump and half turn, startled when someone says excuse me almost in my ear. People keep sneaking up on me today. My elbow nearly hits a fat man on a bicycle trying to get by me. He goes by me peddling fast but going slow. I think his gear is too high. I think I could outrun him. Well, I could have in the old days at least. Today I would probably pull a hamstring or something. Why did he wait to speak until he was on top of me? Did he want to make me jump or is he a dumbass? Maybe it is a reminder that this is not my city. If it were, it would somehow prevent these startling encounters. Does the city remind me that I should get a friend or even a posse to hang around and keep these assholes away from me? Bodyguards would be best. We wouldn't have to be friends and they would keep those bicycles off me. Or have I let things go too long without taking control. Maybe the city is signaling me to clean things up a little; that there are too many loose pieces sticking around, like bacteria left between someone's teeth after a half assed brushing. Across the walk, a filthy man on another bicycle speeds by. I ought to remember to stay alert outside, keep my head on a swivel. It is an important skill when avoiding people. I wonder if anyone asks the guy on the bicycle for a cigarette. I wonder if anyone asks him for his bicycle because I am willing to bet that he doesn't really need it. I wonder if it's even his bicycle. Although cheaper than a car, they aren't that cheap. He probably stole it or maybe borrowed it. In any case, that guy appears to have somewhere important to go. It seems that the people who look like they have the least on their agendas and the most time to accomplish those things are in the biggest hurry to get there. Since I already took a leak I don't have much to accomplish at the moment but I am not in much of a hurry to get it done, so I don't need a bicycle. Maybe I should rush a little more. It may discourage people from asking me for money or cigarettes

The greatest majority of the vagabonds riding bicycles are full grown men and some of them pretty old. I have seen very few women and even fewer children riding bikes. I am in the middle of a city, though, so maybe women and children don't ride bikes here. Maybe all of these guys pretend to ride bikes for the exercise but it only takes a little scrutiny to see that bicycles are their only forms of transportation. I do not believe that a bicycle as the main form of transportation is a choice a man makes easily. If the man wants to get around without a car, he has to ask somebody for a ride or take a bus. If everybody is busy or the bus doesn't go there, he could walk. If it's too far or he doesn't want to walk, he has to get a bicycle. I don't think it works very well for life here, though. When he rides a bike to the store to get groceries, how does he get them home? At least on foot he could push them around the city in a shopping cart. If his girlfriend sticks around when he has only a bicycle, how does he take her out? If he works a distance away, how does he get there? Maybe the filthy guy speeding around is headed to work. If so, it isn't a white collar job, unless he has his work clothes on under his filthy t-shirt and jeans. Maybe he is in disguise as a filthy bum and will rip off his outer rags to reveal clean and tidy professional attire, like Superman. That isn't very likely. Though he acts all proud to be on one, unless he is wearing one of those dorky cyclist outfits, a guy riding a bicycle is signaling that he is down and out. He has no car or no license to drive one. To me, a guy on a bike says OUI. He doesn't have to be really ashamed of it, but he doesn't have to be so proud of it that he speeds around like he is his own trophy, either. It happens to everyone.

It was raining hard when she and I left the house of our friends that night. We had left at a reasonable hour, we thought. It wasn't much later than midnight anyway. Reasonable is all relative. My job was to drive her home without incident as swiftly and safely as possible. Her job was to ride in comfort and allow me to carry her home swiftly and safely. She was my ward, my charge, my precious package. We weren't talking during the ride because the radio was too loud for that. I'm not sure if it was so loud that we couldn't talk or so that we wouldn't. Maybe she was all talked out after visiting with our friends. Or maybe we were in trouble even then. Rebecca liked the music loud anyway, especially when she had been drinking. As we approached the end of the merge ramp, the headlights of oncoming traffic on the highway were distorted by the rain. That was going to make my job harder. All of the traffic in the middle of the night during a monsoon should have made me more careful or suspicious, but with all of the socializing that night, my guard was down. I made the plan to merge into the slow lane traffic until I could get enough speed to move into the faster lane. With the distortion from the rain I didn't realize that I was going faster than the slow cars, so when I merged, I had to move to the next lane more quickly than I had planned. I cut into the middle and then the fast lane pretty quickly, partially blinded by the kaleidoscopic glare of all the headlights through the rain. I didn't have any trouble seeing all of the lights, just the distance and the details. I surely didn't hear any horns blowing. After I had gotten by all of the cars throwing off glittering shafts of random lights and escaped from the trap of headlights, I had no trouble seeing the distance and details of the police lights in the rearview mirror. Had visibility been better, I may have seen that one of the cars that I cut in front of in the fast lane was a state police cruiser. That explained the traffic. A cop on the highway always causes cars to bunch up. When drivers like me see the police car, we slow down to the speed limit and wait for some sucker to pass us and get pulled over. I'll bet it made all of the other drivers kind of glad to see the sucker speed by with the police on his tail that night.

When the trooper ordered me to get out and walk to the back of the car, I knew that I was being arrested for Operating Under the Influence. I knew that I to go through the procedure first, like an elaborate dance, so I obeyed that order. I declined to obey the orders to touch my nose and ears, recite the alphabet and a poem, do a heel-toe walk and the chicken dance. He would have to settle for the familiar four observations that every report gets when the cop wants to pin an OUI on somebody: odor of alcohol, bloodshot eyes, slurred speech and stumble when walking. I simply stood beside the highway in the wind driven rain with my hair plastered to my forehead. I was not happy when the trooper yelled and screamed for a while, berating me for my driving performance. It must be a new part of the procedure. I didn't know I would have to go through that. I thought of how dogs behave. One dog will look down while the other displays dominance. I determinedly looked at the ground and said nothing. I felt a little embarrassed and sort of ridiculous, but the procedure must be followed. I was pretty sure he was going for a reaction so he could have something more than the familiar four to put in his report. It was probably videotaped from the police car and he was going for a reaction for the film. The film always disappears if the guy getting arrested doesn't make a hapless blunder like falling down or taking a swing at the cop. Maybe he wanted Rebecca to see that he could yell and scream at me all he wanted because I wasn't shit. Would a real man allow this kind of treatment, especially in front of his woman? No, but I would. It was hard to make out the yelling in that storm with the cars occasionally whooshing by us. Maybe he was berating me for my lack of judgment. If he wasn't, he should have been. He cuffed my hands behind me and put me in the backseat of his cruiser. I sat on my manacled hands looking through the slightly smeared plexiglass that separated the back seat from the front wondering what was going to become of Rebecca. She was stuck in the car by the highway in a rainstorm. She would not be foolish enough to drive now, even if the police permitted it. As I sat, painfully perched on my twisted hands, I wanted to be near her, to reassure her and be comforted by her. I suppose that my reassurance would seem pretty empty to her if I were able to give it. Being comforted would help me a lot, though.

I felt the same while handcuffed to a bench inside the state police barracks and when a second policeman gathered my fingerprints, mug shot and personal information. The one who arrested me had disappeared, presumably to change his wet clothes and sit by a fire or something. The second policeman disappeared, presumably to comfort the first one after his ordeal, replaced by a third whose duty was apparently to mock me and bait me into incriminating actions or statements that would give the cops something good to use against me in court. It seemed pretty easy and enjoyable for them to push somebody around who was virtually helpless. My actions were limited, being handcuffed to the bench. I had to watch my mouth, though. When he got tired of picking on me and disappeared, I was free to sit shackled and soaked on the unforgiving wooden bench, feeling sorry for myself and wondering what had happened to the love of my life. I had failed in my job of getting her home swiftly and safely. I hoped she was not stuck somewhere, alone and stranded outside a closed service station or in the office of a seedy roadside motel. I couldn't believe that she would just go home and leave me there to figure it out on my own. It would have made it easier sitting on that bench in handcuffs had she and I been talking and laughing together in the car before I was pulled over. We had done that so often before and I missed it. She once told me the amusing story of her former boyfriend who borrowed her car. Well, she didn't have a car at the time, so he borrowed her father's car from her. He had gotten good and impaired with booze and marijuana before he drove over someone's lawn and into their garden gnomes while being followed by a police car. It was one of those slow-speed chases that are so funny when somebody like Seth Rogen does it in a stupid comedy. A very amusing episode. Would she look back on our episode with amusement? Does she tell a current boyfriend about the hijinks we got up to leading to that roadside comedy? I was pretty sure I would not look back with amusement. Where was she?

She was in the prisoner pick up area when a different trooper let me out of the booking room. She had been at the police barracks the whole time. Rather than leave her beside the highway in the early morning, a trooper had brought her there. She had to stay in the waiting room, except for when she had to go pee. Then she had to go outside in the rain and into the bushes because the police wouldn't let her use their bathroom. It rankled as much as being berated by a cop in the rain. That could have been the worst part of the ordeal; she was not deemed worthy to use the ladies room. I cursed the police for abusive tyrants lording their power over a blameless passenger and robbing her of a little dignity. I shared the blame. Worse, the blame was mine because I knew what they would do if we fell into their hands, and I allowed it to happen. OK. If I am forced to admit it, I caused it. I knew they would treat us like enemies, like prisoners of war. At least they didn't beat the bottom of her feet with night sticks or water-board her. Nearly as bad, my sweetheart had to piss in the woods like a dirty vagrant because I had driven like a drunken lunatic with no one in his care. I thought the cops were punishing me by treating her so poorly. I was the only one who thought that, though. She thought they were punishing her because of me. They thought they were punishing her on her own, as an enemy, since I was already being punished. I think that they did not find her all that blameless. I bet those cops would have liked to arrest her too but she wasn't doing anything for which she could be arrested. Maybe they could have nabbed her for pissing outside but they didn't want to go out in the rain. She had only been drinking and, though that isn't illegal, anyone who has been drinking has violated something, maybe a moral law, and is prey for them. It is a perfect double standard because I have known plenty of cops who got so drunk at a bar that they could not function, except to drive to the liquor store on the way home. It's funny that I have never heard about any of them getting busted for OUI. In the minds of the cops, I'm sure, she deserved everything she got and more. No indignity could be too low. She was just a scumbag who drank, kicked canes from under the elderly and molested innocent children. She was an efficient one though, because when I finally came into the waiting area, she had arranged our transportation home. We could not get our car because it had been towed somewhere. Though it had taken a couple of hours, she had acted pretty quickly in calling her friends to come get her and me from jail. That portion of my ordeal was over. If I were a professional athlete or a movie star, I would be all over the news. Everyone in the world would judge and condemn me for actions that had almost destroyed our society with maniacal and savage behavior. Instead, only Rebecca was left to judge and condemn me. I don't know her verdict because she never shared her judgment with me. I suspect it was not favorable.

CHAPTER SIXTEEN

There is a guy with fishing lines dropped in the canal. He has a couple of poles leaning against the handrail and he looks through a tackle box on the walkway next to him. He pores through the little drawers in the box choosing something and then something else. He looks like a regular guy, dressed in a polo shirt and khaki shorts that aren't filthy. When I get close enough, I see that he is a teenager. I don't stop but walk by glancing at his poles and lines and the box he goes through. I don't know what he is doing. He could be from somewhere else, a place where people fish in the rivers. Maybe he's role playing like little kids do when they play tea party or cowboys and Indians. He can't really be fishing. What kind of fish are in the canal? Are there even any fish in there? Maybe he could catch a withered little catfish that washed off the rocks submerged in the dark water. Maybe a frog. Maybe a leech. I'm not sure that I want to see what he drags up from the shallow depths of that filthy trough. It might be fascinating, though. I hear that catfish eat the scum from the bottom of ponds. I also hear they are in the southland and the canal isn't a pond. I hear that some people flush alligators and crocodiles down the toilet when they don't want them any longer. Maybe he can catch an alligator. Maybe he can catch a plastic bag that used to hold a sandwich or a Styrofoam cup with cigarette butts in it. Maybe he is just getting out of the house and he is doing this instead of standing on the street corner looking like he's up to no good.

What is going on? As I walk around this city in the heat and the sun alone with all of these people and my wandering mind, something begins to put a little pressure on the inside of my body. I am getting pulled somewhere. I think I am caught in a paradox. I am pulled, but all toward the center, nothing outward. I feel it in my stomach. Dread begins to grip my stomach and more than that, too. It constricts my intestines like I am tensing my muscles, all of them. It's in my chest, as if I jogged up the slope of the tiny hill leading here. I can feel it in my arms and hands like I have just lifted an invisible pail of water. It is even in my legs making me want to sit on a bench and rest them. But I don't want to sit because the dread inside of me tightens a little at a time like shoelaces binding everything under my skin and I must move. There is nothing to dread but I feel it anyway. I am animated by necessity, not energy. I am a wooden marionette imbued with the compulsion to move. Not Pinocchio. He could think and talk and grow and lie. More like the broom in 'The Nutcracker' that just moves. I move slowly because the dread that compels me binds me at the same time as it animates me. I am paralyzed in motion. I have no place to go, but I am going there. I am coming from nothing, but remember all of it. I am living death while I am dying. Dante did not create Heaven, Hell and Purgatory, I did. I created Purgatory but I am the only one in it. I will walk uphill no matter what the terrain, like Sisyphus pushing his boulder in Tartarus, purging my sins and mistakes as I go until they all are addressed and answered and rectified. Then maybe God will talk to me again and tell me what I can do to make everything all right and also make no more mistakes. Am I becoming better making no new mistakes and wrestling with the old ones and everything I regret while my insides tingle and contract with the shoelace tightening dread? But the paradox reigns and I can't tell what the nature of my mistakes were. Was everything a mistake or was everything a calculation? What was an adventure and what was a blunder? What started as an adventure and finished as an error? Did I lie and say I made a mistake when it all came out wrong? Would I say I meant to do it if everything came out right? I know in my heart that whatever came out right was a mistake too. The things that were happy at first turned hopeless during or after the act. Was anything I ever did correct? Somehow I made everything disperse. I can't sit, but I sit. I am still moving spasmodically inside, tumultuously grappling with despair while immobile. I vow that I am going to take control of myself.

I sit. Time passes. I am Rip Van Winkle. I have come the distance from my home and rested here. I could picture nothing but happiness and now I can't remember it. I do not sleep. I can hear the rumble and noise of passing trucks and cars from far away. I am alone. Rumble and noise comes from inside of me emitting into the atmosphere. An invisible cloud looms above. My clothes are new yet outdated. They come from various relationships long ago when love, togetherness and hope were in the world. My skin is supple yet sags on my face and my hands. It, too, came from a prior relationship. My hair is shaggy yet receding. It grows or goes away of its own volition whenever and wherever it chooses. My shoes have broken through on the sides and worn through on the bottom. They are the foundation that supports my every step. Technology has passed me by. I can't live without it yet I can't comprehend it. On a bench that no homeless man sleeps on or behind I sit awake in my own dream watching nothing. I think of nothing because that is the most important thing in the whole world. Twenty years pass while I watch empty air that holds nothing. The sun never sets and the wind never rises. I am in the same spot that I was long ago and nothing has changed except everything. All of the half visible people around me do not exist. I sit in a whirlpool going around and around but always heading toward the hole. I reside there. Sometimes high on the edge and sometimes close to the center, everything is lighter and then darker but no progress. I have no apathy. I will take control of myself.

I rise. I look at the clock on the city hall spire. Seven minutes have passed since the fat man passed me on his bicycle. I don't want to walk around anymore. Tough shit, I guess. It's still sunny, it's still hot, I'm still sweating out beer and I'm closer to the river than to my place. Where do I want to be less, the river park or my apartment? I'll take the river. I'm just about at the old building converted into a restaurant that sits at the confluence of five streets. It's a fairly large restaurant and a big place for a house but not a big place for a factory. I assume it was originally someone's house, but I don't have time for that now. I am in a hurry to get to the river. I am now an aimless sweaty guy with nothing on my agenda and in a big hurry to accomplish it.

I walk at a brisk pace, I think, past the restaurant on the right, the sprawling police station across the street on the left and the High School on the right. I cross the street and walk around an arena to the tiered park behind. There is the river-walk path; that's where I want to be. There are dozens of guys wearing police t-shirts on the lawn between the Arena and the river-walk. They are apparently being trained in methods to subdue a sloppy drunk. An instructor demonstrates on a volunteer the proper way to approach a perp while he is face down on the ground, put a knee in his back and bend his arm behind him while keeping the elbow locked and the wrist twisted. Oh good. A bunch of bullies who were unpopular in school are being trained to brutalize anyone who doesn't obey their orders and then call him the perpetrator. Yet, if the perp is face down on the ground with his arms spread, isn't he obeying orders already? Or maybe he has just been tazed and is helpless for a few moments. I wonder if the instructor is going to demonstrate reading the volunteer his Miranda rights or apologizing for overreacting and going too far. I go to a bench down the lawn and away, mostly isolated, and I huddle into my little smoking moment: me, myself, my embarrassment and remorse. I will figure out what to do to take control.

CHAPTER SEVENTEEN

Mistakes mistakes mistakes mistakes. Bloopers blunders failures sins. Damned. That's all fiction too. There are always mistakes to be made. Everything is a mistake made by somebody. If you get a good deal at an open-air market, the seller made a mistake. If you get a bad deal, you made one. If you read a book and don't like it, is it your mistake or the writer's? If you bump into a guy at the street corner, one of you made a mistake. I'm not the only one in my life to make mistakes. Whose mistake was it when I went through the bar and punched Peter in the head a couple of times, knocking him on his ass? Peter's, that's who. All right. Mine too, but at least he was the one who got knocked on his ass. He knew Lynn as well as I did, maybe better. OK. Better. They had been friends for years before I met her. They were sleeping together, I guess periodically, while he was married with a couple of kids and she had a long-time boyfriend. I didn't know anything about that when she and I moved in together. After we were together for a while, I didn't put any stock in it when a few people told me a thing about them here and another thing there. It was in the distant past. I thought I was in charge of that relationship, but I was mistaken. Lynn was very attentive and very possessive, like I was the last individually wrapped mint in the bowl at a party where they served garlic dip. It was pretty flattering, really.

She got me the clothes she wanted me to wear so that I would look right when people saw us together.

She pushed her views on me so that I would adopt them and I would then voice the opinions she held whenever I talked to others. We visited her parents on weekends and holidays or her family in another state for extended weekends. Always together, we went to whatever parties she chose where someone would invariably ask when we were getting married. Lynn would say to ask me and, to her chagrin, I would say that I didn't know. We went out with her friends, which worked out all right because we all worked together and so I worked with most of them anyway. Though we worked with Peter too, he became a friend of mine through other people not her. He was pretty funny sometimes. Like when a bunch of the guys went deep sea fishing and he got so sick that we had to carry him to his van and drive him home. When his wife met us at the door, we all had a good laugh because he was the big fisherman in our group and he had organized the excursion. Lynn didn't talk to him much and even acted like she didn't like him. I learned about their previous intimacy through some innocuous comments and discussions among friends. Everyone was so casual about it that I didn't think very deeply about it. I do recall telling him in jest one time that she was with me now and the two of them were all finished. I thought it was funny at the time. I always figured that with all of the attention she paid to me, she would have no time for anyone else. With all of that attention, it was actually me who had no time for anyone else.

One New Year's Eve at our place on the third floor of an old warehouse on the river that had been converted into apartments, we were sharing the celebration with two of my brothers and their girlfriends. One brother mentioned shaving his head. The other brother jumped on that, volunteering to help with an eagerness that was contagious. Without taking it seriously, I joined in happily. The girls giggled dismissively at such an idea. We joked about it for a while until, urged on by their skepticism, our willingness and possibly champagne, my brother decided it was a good idea. We had scissors, a plastic disposable razor, a bathtub and my brother's nicely coifed head when we went into the bathroom while Lynn and the other girls stayed in the living room scoffing at the idea. I laughed when my brother stripped naked and squatted in the tub, his knees at his chest and his ass touching the bottom. I thought nothing could be funnier, but I was wrong. It was funnier and I laughed harder when one brother clipped the hair off the head of the other. An accidental clip or two of the scalp elicited mild ouches, nothing more. It got even funnier and I laughed even harder when one of them had shaved the head of the other until there were random patches of stubble on the top and back of his mangy-looking head. It looked like little odd-shaped patches of hair had fallen from a top shelf onto his bald head and some had stuck onto it. There was more hair clinging to his testicles touching the traction strips on the bottom of the tub between his heels as he squatted naked while snickering at the great joke we were sharing. We were laughing so hard that it was impossible to finish the shave job. One brother was squatting naked in the bathtub with a few little tufts of hair clinging to the top, sides and back of his head. The other was clutching his abdomen with scissors and a razor, paralyzed with laughter. There was no hooting and hollering; there was gasping and wheezing with hilarity that was nearly painful in intensity. A pounding on the door added to it for a moment, like the little room became full of thumping from my veins keeping time with the throb of our laughter. Soon though, an angry voice wormed into my awareness.

Someone was pounding on the door telling us to stop it. She was demanding we unlock the door and asking what was wrong with us. Our laughter dwindled to snickers. Then it evaporated as she kept hitting the door accusing us of being sick and having sex in the bathroom. I opened the door and there was Lynn, crying with anger and jealousy. The other girls were in the living room staring fixedly at the very interesting events unfolding on TV. Our New Year's party was over, as the ball fell in Times Square on the television. Nobody wanted to stick around for our argument, including me. During the escape, Lynn clung to my waist shrieking about love and togetherness as we all got out the door onto the landing in the hallway. We couldn't see the eyes at the peepholes and ears to the doors of the other apartments that shared the landing and the hallway. When our door closed and the automatic lock clicked, we were stuck, locked on the landing surrounded by neighbors listening to Lynn scream for me to stay with her and don't leave. We were able to get her inside when my brother kicked in the door while I ran barefoot down two flights of stairs into the icy streets on the first night of our new year.

Waking on New Year's Day at my brother's house was at first a fairly depressing new beginning. I knew I had to go home to Lynn and find out what she had waiting for me. It became a little less depressing when I watched my brother walk around the corner, gently nurturing my little niece, his daughter. She needed it because she was confused and frightened by him. He had walked right out of my nightmare into our waking day. He had the good-mood face as always, but his head was a little monstrous. He had a glowing white scalp with angry new scabs over the razor nicks here and there. There were some tufts of black hair stuck on the back of his head like little Velcro fasteners. It was the bad dream illuminated by a light that shows the dream isn't really bad, it's just the shadows in your mind skewing the dream into a scary angle. I could not help laughing out loud.

I decided to make a change in my life after a neighbor, a psychologist, recommended that I go to counseling to control my anger issues. After hearing the uproar in the hallway on New Year's Eve, and apparently talking to Lynn, she figured that I had a problem leading to all of the violence in my relationship. That summer we moved to a different apartment. I stopped working with Lynn and the rest of the crowd to begin at another place. She still worked with Peter, though. We were all still friends, but our schedules altered slightly so her tardiness sometimes was easy to explain. Lynn would ask me if we were going to get married, I would say not at the moment, and she would be late to get home or to meet all of us later that night or that week. Someone would make a veiled comment about she and Peter and I would brush it aside saying what she said; that it isn't a big deal because we were together and she was too faithful to do anything inappropriate with anyone else. Someone else told me in confidence that she was with Peter and I said fine, she told me that they were talking. She was devoted to me and we were all friends. Someone else told me that he saw her on the floor with Peter late one night after hours. It was so dark that he couldn't be certain exactly what was going on but the motions suggested that she was not being particularly devoted. I suppose I had to do something. I wasn't convinced that there was anything that could split us, but every single other person I knew saw more than I did. She and I discussed our relationship again and again, though we never discussed Peter, and finally decided that my move to a different apartment might give us space enough to clarify what was becoming muddled in our life. We no longer lived together, but we were working it through. We would talk about how to repair our thing or make it better. I was at her apartment that used to be ours one afternoon. We talked for a while, held hands, then hugged and kissed. It was possible everything would work out all right. After our sweat began to mingle, but before our sighs of contentment, the phone rang and the answering machine took the call. It was Peter calling to ask Lynn what she was doing and did she want to get together for a while. He could come over. My mood flipped from amorous to callous and no sigh of contentment came that day. Everything everyone hinted or said was true.

Over the course of the following weeks, she would ask whenever she had an opportunity if we were going to get married. I would then ask if she was going to stop seeing Peter. She never answered that question but she did say that he always liked and wanted her. Who wouldn't, I wondered, but he had hidden it pretty well for quite a while. She called me frequently and always asked me to call back. When I called her at work and Peter answered, he thought that I should know that Lynn, over the years, had always taken the initiative when they got together. Every time. This was a contradiction to everything she had told me, most of which was that nothing happened until I moved out and left her. It also seemed like a contradiction to the call I heard when she and I were in a passionate embrace. I was suddenly humiliated and angry. Was I being mocked for the condition of my heart? Was I such a contemptible figure, so ridiculous, that they dared to lie so transparently and tell me such different versions of the same story? That story was that the two of them were together and I was out, clinging to the disintegrating fringe of our indestructible relationship. Maybe I was trying to grasp an illusion, but was I such a fool that I would take it like a clown who gets a pie in the face every show? I had to take action and put a stop to the indecisive behavior that was causing such an intolerable situation to continue. My inaction was causing constant doubt and confusion. Hmm. What to do, what to do? On the spur of the moment, I decided to illustrate that I had perhaps been a fool, but I was not the type of fool they were taking me for. Truthfully, though, I had already half decided a long time before what I would do. I said to him, right, OK, I will be there in a minute.

I went to the bar that Peter was tending and where Lynn was working, walked behind it and told him I came to see him and not Lynn because I was going to beat his ass. To his credit, he didn't flinch. He said, Yeah? Do it then. I did it. They weren't my hardest punches and I delivered them without vicious intent. I wanted to hurt him then; I didn't want to kill him. I wanted to vent my anger and let him and everyone else know that I was finished with being tugged along behind them like a quadriplegic in a little wagon. Also to his credit, he didn't lose consciousness. When he attempted to duck under the blows, I missed his chin and hit him in the temple and the cheek. He stumbled back into the bottles on the wall and wobbled around bleary for a moment before he slumped down and hit his ass on the floor. He righted himself and made a half-crouch stumbling charge forward to grab my waist. He probably wanted to tackle me but his energy was drained from the struggle to stay on his feet. Meanwhile, Lynn was screaming like someone was smashing her fingers with a hammer. I didn't know if she was screaming for him or for me. Was she screaming at me? Maybe she was another pacifist and my violence was causing her pain. Violence does seem to affect those pacifists in strange ways. Her screams brought a bunch of people, some from the bar, animated out of the shock that my scene had created. Some came from the street or from the ether or from who knows where. They converged on us and pushed between us, grabbing, separating, holding. I was thankful for their arrival because Peter was mostly helpless and I didn't want to hit him anymore. They held us firmly wrapped in their hands and arms so that we couldn't get free and continue the brawl. They held him firmly anyway. It was a good idea because he wasn't too steady on his feet. They were a lot less firm with me. Several guys held Peter while one guy restrained me with a hand. One hand was enough, though. I didn't want to hurt my good friend.

There were certainly mistakes, and at the time I didn't think they were mine. That was one of my biggest errors. I said that the biggest mistake I made was putting trust in people who were not trustworthy. I said that I wasn't quick enough in demonstrating my independence. I said that I had been too pliable from the beginning. But that was all my way of shifting the blame to someone else. Saying that I didn't know what Lynn wanted was a lie. She made it clear enough. If she pressured me too much and too soon, like I said then, it was my fault for giving a false presentation. But, then, I kind of liked the attention. I think the closest I ever got to being honest about my culpability was when I admitted that perhaps I didn't propose marriage quickly enough. I just refused to let myself go and become committed to something. If her expectations were unreasonable it was because she didn't understand my flaw. In a way, to my shame, I led her on. I suspect that if I had been properly nurturing, if I were committed to her and our relationship, things would have worked out. She had a flaw too, though. She was attracted to another man but she didn't want to let me go. She wanted us both and thought she could have us both. She figured she could manipulate me even more that she already had and coerce me into proposing marriage by having another fling with the guy. Lynn thought she could hook up with Peter again and use my indecision as an excuse. I would then take the blame, beg her to be mine forever, and feel guilty for driving her to be with another man. She even admitted her secret plan later. Not the hooking up with another man part. She would never admit to that. The coercion part; that she admitted. If she meant that, she may have been right all along about the two of being the same. It looks like we both lied to ourselves. I am sure that she waited for me to commit to something and I could not do it. I am sure she got fed up with me taking the same tack party after party, time after time and began to look around. I think she got bored with waiting for me to take action and she moved on to something more interesting.

I made another mistake, too. I didn't make Peter pay a high enough price for the part he played in our drama. I thought he had betrayed our friendship. I figured that he assumed I was more passive than I was and he expected there would be no repercussions for ignoring me, taking my relationship away and flaunting it. He didn't even bother asking for it.

Whatever was mine was his for the taking. He may have thought he was safe staying in public while he made a fool of me. Maybe he just wanted something that I had and he felt he deserved. He had set it aside for a while, like a selfish bum who quits smoking until a guy with cigarettes passes by. Maybe he didn't care if I were passive or aggressive because I was of no consequence. Only Lynn was. There was a little satisfaction in knocking him bleary, not a lot. If I had really hurt him, I may have felt a little worse about it then, but I would feel a lot better about it now. Again it boils down to my lack of follow-through. I could have fixed something broken right then had I taken care of it more thoughtfully and thoroughly. Back then, I had a lot to learn about being in control of my situation.

CHAPTER EIGHTEEN

I sit on the mostly isolated bench under the branches of a fairly young tree. It is maybe four inches in diameter, so it was planted long after the city ceased to be a productive manufacturing center. I cannot see the thugs up on the lawn as they practice arm-bars, leg-sweeps and wrist-locks to subdue hard-core underage drinkers and elderly smart mouth jaywalkers. There are occasional walkers and bicycle riders on the river walk above and to the left of my bench. They can look down and see me here if they choose. These bicyclists are different from the ones in the city itself. These look like recreational riders or college students. They are younger and wear more preppy looking clothes than the tattered old guys in the DTL. Some even wear the ridiculous cycling outfit complete with that idiotic helmet. The proximity to the college makes a lot of difference. I wonder if the police trainees eye them with the longing of bulldogs watching bunnies walk or bicycle past. The river-walk is newer than the basin where I sit. There are three very large culverts with caps over the mouths embedded in the small hillside to my right. They look like big walk-in vaults stuck into the hill with wooden bench seats built on them for a disguise. This area was obviously a discharge basin into the Merrimack River for some of the old manufacturing waste. I envision foamy creamy brownish liquid gushing out of the tubes with enough force to push anything in its path into the river. Volumes of dyes, formaldehyde, sulfate, mercury and other things mixed with water to form a liquid that wore the ground away in a wide muddy u-shaped swath from the culverts to the river. It probably smelled like rotten eggs and rancid poultry. The grass on the edge of the torrent that wasn't ripped away with the soil was poisoned with chemicals. When the rush of the water from the discharge tubes diminished until it was a moderate flow, and finally to a trickle, the muddy earth was sloped toward the river enough to funnel the oozing mixture into it. The culverts are sealed now. The capped mouths look like and perhaps serve the function of vaults, securing and hiding secrets that could be discovered in the pipes that lead to the bowels of the city. I bet some very dark secrets reside behind those vault covers. When the river-walk was built it formed a wall between the river and this cozy little isolated garden spot. The river bank is closer to the river-walk here than other places, probably an example of what 100 or so years of shooting toxic waste out of gigantic hoses can do to a riverbank. I wonder what toxic residue is beneath the ground where I sit. I expect there are some textile treatment chemicals down there, probably with cancerous isotopes that have a half-life of eight million years. Everything has its dirty secrets, I suppose.

I knew Rebecca had secrets when we began spending time together. Our first date was on a beautiful beach day. We met at a closed ice cream shop on a secondary road behind a little stand of trees. She said it was more convenient and better for parking than if I picked her up. She didn't say anything about her family or friends seeing me pick her up. On our next date, we met at a place in a nearby town to see a band. Neither of us had ever heard of the band or knew anyone in the town, but that wasn't important. Then she came to my town to go out because it was fun and different to get away. Then a night away somewhere. After a while, I started to wonder if she was an orphan of the world without any friends or family. I never pried because we were together to have a good time and we were doing that. Her private matters were none of my business. I said I didn't care about it, but that wasn't really true. The truth was that I may have already lost my heart to her and I cared a lot. I didn't admit that, of course, not even to myself. Although we eventually had to meet each other's people if we were going to spend so much time together, I found myself becoming a little impatient with the delay. I missed my family and friends, but I wanted to spend my time with her, so I began bringing her with me to do things with them. It was kind of frustrating how long it took for her to introduce me to anyone she knew. Was I the secret from the rest of her life, or was the rest of her life a secret from me? As time went on, I told myself that those secrets weren't greatly important because I was being a modern, more sophisticated man. Except when we were scheduled to be together and she was late. I was then a primitive, more jealous crank. It made me feel like I was insignificant to her. I figured I held the number three boyfriend slot to her. She probably had someone she called her boyfriend. That would be the one she went out with in public and brought to family functions. Then I expected that she had a number two. He must be the guy she dated when her boyfriend was busy and she wanted to do something. He wouldn't get to go to family things, but he was in line to be number one when she and the boyfriend split up. I would be number three, in line for the number two slot. She would keep me around just for fun. I never knew anything for certain. Maybe she wasn't really secretive, just private. I wouldn't want to disparage her without any facts or anything. And anyway, how can one person assume what another's secrets are? I don't know, but I did it anyway.

She was able to compartmentalize things better than anyone I had known before. I was tolerant, even indulgent, and able to ignore uncomfortable possibilities better than ever before in my life. I made a conscious decision to avoid making the mistakes I had made in my past relationships. I would not repeat the mistakes I made with Lisle or Lucy, Alicia or Helen. Seldom did I allow possessiveness or jealousy to gestate and become substantial. I would scold it and ridicule it. I would make my jealousy feel embarrassment for even existing. She had a life before me, even during my emergence in her life, and I didn't want her to give it all up or lose it. I refused to repeat the blunders I had made with Patricia or Lynn. I wanted her to maintain her friendships. I thought that if we had only one another and no one else, we would not be able to last forever. If she counted on me and my life to keep her entertained and interested, she would grow bored pretty quickly. If she kept everything that was pleasant in her life like friends, hobbies, activities, even times out at bars or nightclubs, she would still be who she was when I fell for her. The constant tiny sliver of doubt that I always had was good. It would always keep me aware of our relationship and how important it was. I was on the verge of actually being the contemporary Renaissance man. I was going to be modern and liberal and accepting. I was going to like myself. I was ready.

Of course, I didn't mean boyfriends or lovers, but how would I be able to tell? They were all strangers to me. I was, in fact, a stranger to them as well. How can a stranger distinguish between someone else's friend and lover, especially if the two have never actually met? How could somebody know who anybody was if he was just a stranger on the other side of a room? I think that a stranger cannot distinguish between friends, enemies, family, work associates, arms dealers, investors, partners in crime, clients, drug suppliers or other strangers. It must, then, become a matter of trust. I made a decision to trust her and I promised myself that I would live by that. This was how I would exercise control over our situation; I would trust her. I liked myself even more. I would not be the cause of our destruction by becoming a suspicious and overbearing partner. I wanted her to want to be with me because she liked it. I would never make threats, display violence or let jealousy rule. I would not bring the trouble into our lives that those behaviors invited. Besides, do I want someone to stay with me because she is intimidated by me or fears me? Will terror make her be more loyal to me or love me more than she does without it? I am sure there have been lots of frightened women who were not deterred from stepping out on their partner/overseer due to fear. I wanted no fear to pervade my sweetheart's thoughts. Not if I was going to be the new living Renaissance man. I wanted every feeling and desire to be freely given and mutual. It had to be freely given or I didn't want it. I vowed that I would be an enlightened and progressive man. That was the vow by which I promised to live and that was the vow I adhered to when Rebecca's friend, a guy I had met a couple of times, called to tell me that she couldn't come home that night because she was too drunk to drive.

When she texted me earlier in the afternoon to say that she would be home soon darling, I was glad. I was always glad when she came home. I looked forward to it. She was cozy and comfortable like home but inside my chest. It may be true that home is where the heart is. I just liked her around. Maybe it was a chemical reaction because even when she was sleeping I loved her presence. One of my favorite things ever in life was watching her sleep. She was lovely even with her spectacular eyes closed, but more peaceful. I felt good about the world when I was able to see her at such peace and I was glad to be a part of it. What could be bad in the world if she was so tranquil? She had a trusting vulnerability, an innocence that she didn't have when awake. I liked everyone and everything during those moments. If I was the person she wanted, then I was the person I wanted to be.

She texted later in the afternoon to say that she would be home a little later than she had thought. She had met a friend somewhere. I wasn't exactly disappointed, but I wasn't as glad as before. When she texted that evening to say that she would be home later because they had gone to someplace, I was disappointed. Maybe even annoyed. When she didn't text that night to tell me where she was or when she would be home, I became mostly worried and a little angry. It was a good thing I had been practicing all of that time with that little sliver of doubt so I had some toughness built up, because when the night verged on morning and I had failed to reach her with texts and calls, her friend Mike called on her phone to tell me that Rebecca couldn't make it home. Where was she? She was OK. Where exactly was that? Oh. Uh, she was safe at his house but she was pretty loaded and I really wouldn't want her to drive home in that condition. I wouldn't? He may have been right about that, but how would he know what I wanted? He called me using her phone to tell me what I wanted. I wanted to know where he lived because I would be right over to get her. Huh? Well, um, never mind. He would drive her home. She would be there in a little while. No, really. She was home in a little while.

CHAPTER **NINETEEN**

Standing at the rail on the river-walk is lovely. The Merrimack River is right at my feet. The current seems fairly swift, but I have no frame of reference. I don't know how swiftly it should run. Several ducks are down in the river and on the bank. They swim and dip their beaks into the water, bobbing around like they can't control their direction. The current is not running so swiftly that it carries the ducks away, so they must be in control. They look pretty social and happy to be together. They are a somewhat soothing sight. Unperturbed by the current, the heat and the people who watch them, like me. They just swim and bob around. The ducks are unaffected by temperature, weather, flotsam and debris. The protection they get from their feathers must be as effective as wearing a spacesuit. Or they could just be tough. During the cold months, they swim around in the canals between sheets of ice that cover much of the water. It makes them seem indestructible. Maybe I shouldn't have laughed so loudly when I heard of the pro hockey team named the Mighty Ducks. The swimming ducks appear to be bothered by nothing. They swim and mill around together all happy like there aren't any predators, partnerships or problems. Maybe there aren't, but how can you tell with a bunch of tough ducks that have unfathomable emotions? Maybe the duck bobbing around in the water is pissed off at the duck on the bank because she talked to another duck while he was out on the river. He looks mild to me because his beak is stuck in an upturned position which I think looks like a smile, but the other ducks know it's a grimace. Maybe there are a few bum ducks irritating the energetic ducks by continually asking for a saturated cigarette butt or something. When I look down at them, I can't tell which is an asshole duck and which is a considerate duck. Would they have an argument in duck talk where one tells the other to stop acting like a damned human being? Would it be better for the ducks if some of them, the undesirables who drag them down, were hunted down and cut out of the group? Since they don't have any claws, teeth or any way to hold a weapon, I assume they have no way to purge the social group. One duck really can't do anything to threaten another duck. If the ducks want one of them gone, they must just turn their backs on him. That's no guarantee that the asshole duck will go away. They can't get rid of their repugnant social misfit; they are stuck with the little shit. Being indestructible has some drawbacks. Maybe the ducks aren't that happy and accepting. Maybe they are trapped in weakness, burdened with frustration and impotence for their entire indestructible lives. And there is nothing they can do about it.

I wonder if it bothered Rebecca that I didn't do something about that night. It has always bothered me. I wanted to do something, but I didn't want to do the wrong thing. What was her choice and what was coercion? She was always so determined and certain of her actions that I couldn't think of anything that would make her obey another person if she didn't choose to do it. She was not submissive and I didn't think she would be threatened by a friend. She may have thought that I was a coward for not taking action, but I can't think of what action I could have taken. From whom would I demand an account and possibly punish for that night and what would I punish anyone for? If I held Mike responsible, I would have to do something hard and brutal. I didn't know him very well, but I knew he was kind of a giant and confident of his physical abilities. I had him pegged for the kind of guy quick to ask for trouble, bluster in the face of it, and then back down if the situation got dangerous. I figured he would face me because he was big enough, back up when it got serious, and then call the cops when he got hurt. I would have to hurt him quickly to make my statement. If Rebecca was responsible, as I suspected, I was at a loss. That would be just one more of her secrets. Well, since I didn't even know what happened, I suppose it would be two secrets. It would make Mike an innocent culprit and any action I took to punish him would make him a victim. How would I punish her? If she wanted that night to go as it did then I had nothing to say about it except that my feelings were hurt.

Maybe I am like an impotent and indestructible duck with no weapon against her except my toughness. Maybe I am a coward and I use the excuse that I don't want to be that kind of man. I use the excuse that fighting is embarrassing and ridiculous especially for grown men and that it is beneath my dignity, as though my dignity is a real thing. But I have seen grown men fighting and it is an embarrassing sight. Maybe fighting is not the way to display bravery in our peaceful and benevolent society and I don't know what is. Initiating a physical contest may not be a way to show courage, but avoiding one is a way to show cowardice. Another paradox. Maybe she wanted me out of her hair and was giving me a secret signal to run away from home. But I missed the signal and, besides, I've heard that running away from things is cowardly. I should have gone after Mike. If I had, I would at least have done something instead of just waiting, inactive, to see where we were going. I would have made a statement and I could have salvaged a little self-esteem. I wonder if I would have kept some prestige in her eyes. Would that have made the difference? Well, maybe my chance to demonstrate bravery, if I have any, will come again some day. Next time it will all be different. Isn't that what all cowards say when the chance has passed? But I can't go back. I can never go back.

CHAPTER TWENTY

Dignity. It's a good thing I haven't staked my life on that. It is such an important concept to me as I shuffle around all self-absorbed and shabby, like so many of these arrogant slatternly pricks who hate themselves. We all strut or pedal or shuffle around like we know something no one else does, like we are important. We hustle to nowhere, waiting for, even daring, some condescending douchebag to question us or make a comment that we can find offensive. And then we have an excuse to become indignant; to challenge the douchebag and show how much dignity we have. We have as much right to this space, this sidewalk, this city as anyone and we aren't afraid to loudly declaim our right. After all, nobody can lay a finger on us, no matter how disagreeable, crude or inappropriate we are. It's a free country. We are free to be as presumptuous, obnoxious and uncouth as we want. But this is all wrong. We aren't even important in our own minds. Dignity is compromised when we push our shopping carts full of empty cans or bottles or dirty clothes with great energy through the lots and down the sidewalks. The cans and bottles are empty because we drink whatever is in them as soon as we get them. We give away our dignity while we look around and surreptitiously drink beer behind the food-mart or sneak mini-bottles of booze and smoke whatever we can buy or beg or steal. We do it until we stagger or stumble or vomit and then demand respect because it is our due. The perfect example of someone displaying a lack of dignity is a sloppy drunk guy stumbling around while bleeding from where he hit his head on the pavement. It would display a total lack of dignity if he soiled himself while doing it. I would never do that. As Rachel is my witness, I wouldn't.

Rachel liked something about me when we first met. I bet it looked like I had potential and that I was going somewhere. I apparently worked to support myself while going to school. That's what I told everyone. I may even have thought it myself. The truth was that I worked to buy party goods like booze or drugs and I went to school to discover the parties where the co-eds were. Charles and I shared an apartment off campus in the same complex as Rachel. He and I were waiters at a restaurant and had most of our days free to hang around the pool area at the apartment complex. We worked on our tans and made our plans to perfect the playboy lifestyle while we rose to success. Rather than waste time studying, we practiced our dives in the pool, played water volleyball or sat around in the hot-tub drinking beer or rum, whatever the day called for. Rachel was not a co-ed but a professional and, like many of the other professionals living in that complex, she had a daytime job and did not normally get to witness the hard work we devoted to procrastination and underachievement. That was lucky for me because her opinion of me was higher. Because she had a day job, I had to wait until evening whenever I was going to visit her. It worked out because I sometimes had to work and we weren't together every evening. Some nights I didn't have to work but I said I did because I had something else to do.

We met at one of those get-to-know-you functions for residents of the complex. I was struck by the long, straight brown hair that represented her perfectly. Nothing about Rachel was quirky or exaggerated or out of place, except maybe her taste in men. She was pretty in a wholesome professional way, spoke with proper professional grammar and diction and she dressed in conservative professional attire. I liked her dignified style and admired her as I surreptitiously stuffed complimentary cupcakes in my mouth and cheese and crackers in my pockets. She was a nice quiet girl who didn't swear, get sloppy or make scenes. I did that, but I didn't do it when Rachel was around. On some occasions she had girlfriends, no doubt work mates, over to socialize and they were similar to Rachel in their reserved professional demeanors. They would sit by the pool sometimes before going out to do whatever conservative professional girls do. I thought Rachel's friends kept their desire for Charles and me under control by exercising their will-power and because Rachel had already claimed me. I suspect, though, they watched us less with desire than curiosity, like professional administrators would watch monkeys leaping around and acting up in the cages at the zoo.

The front stairs to her apartment were on the patio next to the hot-tub, like they were part of the pool area, so she couldn't sneak by when we were at the pool. At least not by the front stairs. She could sneak up by the back stairs if she wanted, but I don't think she ever did in the beginning. When I was done sunning and swimming and was ready to visit her, it was easy to go right up the front stairs. On a beautiful day like so many others, Charles and I made our plan like so often. The plan was to perform our early day duties, which consisted going to class, going to the liquor store, and then going to the pool. The alternate plan was to skip the class, go to the liquor store and then go to the pool.

I would visit Rachel that evening while Charles went somewhere he was invited, or at least not uninvited. As always, the pool was a great place to wait around for the next work shift, the next party or Rachel. We relaxed in the sun and socialized with other people from the complex. Some of the other students actually went to their classes. We played a few water volleyball games with whomever was interested, some two on two, some five on five. We had a drink-making contest to see who could make the most interesting rum concoction using anything we had or could get. We sat in the hot-tub even though the day was hot. It was so hot that the hot-tub seemed cool at first. After being in it for a while, though, it seemed hotter. That may be what made me slur. We lazed around in the water and we lazed around on the beach chairs. We talked about the heat and politics and current events and sports. After the day of indulging in the toxic combination of sun and rum, people drifted away to their personal appointments, duties or classes and Rachel arrived at the pool area at the expected time.

She talked to Charles while waiting for me at the foot of her stairs. I figured I would go for one more dip in the water and I decided to combine the pool with the hot-tub experience. When I dove into the hot-tub, I thought I was being cool and Rachel would be impressed. I said I did it because it was there. Actually, I did it because my judgment had been drowned in the pool, the hot-tub and the rum. The hot-tub was only about three feet deep and when I dove into it, I crushed my head into the corner where the concrete seat meets the concrete wall. Boy was that a collision. Even loaded I recognized the power of the impact. I saw stars, black spots, swirls, giant question marks and exclamation points like Wile E. Coyote sees in the cartoon when the road runner drops a boulder on him. When I stood up, blood mixed with the chlorinated water flowed down my forehead from where the skin was smashed through to the skull between my crown and forehead. As I crawled out of the hot-tub and stood on weak, rubbery legs, Charles tried to stifle laughter but he didn't do very well because his judgment had also been drowned. Probably because she had just gotten home from work and her judgment was intact, Rachel was kind of horrified. Filled with concern, she helped me stagger up the stairs to her apartment so she could care for my smashed head while I talked her out of calling an ambulance. Rather than send me back to my place, she gave me the best first aid treatment she could before she settled me into her bed. Though I had stayed there in the past, it was never for medical attention or observation and it was an odd feeling being administered to and worried over by this sweet and kind angel from another world. Maybe the odd feeling was from the impact on my skull, who knows?

I don't think it was a fun time for her. It wasn't that much fun for me either, but I was grateful for her effort. I suspect she was not thrilled that she had decided to keep that evening free to enjoy my visit. Maybe I'm just paranoid. As a staid professional, that behavior was not common for her and though she never said so, I believe she was a fairly disturbed, maybe even disgusted. For the next few days, I still felt kind of drunk. While waiting tables, whenever someone told me his order I had to write it down while he spoke or I would not remember. I didn't spend much time at the pool that week so I don't know if Rachel went up the back stairs or what. Or maybe I forgot that, too. I do remember looking down at Rachel as we shared a tender embrace later. Her long brown hair fanned out on the pillow beneath her head and shoulders, framing her pretty professional face and delightful professional shoulders in an exquisite vision of wholesome loveliness. It was such a classic and perfect pose that it could have been created by an artist or photographer. I had never seen her look more enchanting. As I admired her from a foot above, supporting myself with my hands and pelvis in the most intimate moment I ever enjoyed with Rachel, a small drop slowly rolled from my hairline down my forehead, just like any little drop of sweat would during exertion. From the tip of my nose, a drop of clear viscous fluid mingled with a little blood fell to her bare chest. I have the wistful feeling that the drop contained some memory that will not return. Maybe it was something else that was important. I wonder what it was.

The image she had of me was different than the reality. She got a glimpse that day of the kind of a person I was. When she began to watch more closely, Rachel began to understand that I wasn't really working while putting myself through school. I was less focused than that. I was running around looking for the next good time and she was part of it. She probably wanted to spend her time and energy with someone who had goals or at least someone who wouldn't frighten her. How could she take someone to an office party who would potentially get staggering drunk and knock over the buffet table? She wouldn't dare bring a guy to the professional Christmas Party who would try to grab the breast of her female boss or puke on the dance floor. She wasn't looking for someone at the peak of success, just someone she could rely on for emotional support and to not embarrass her. Or maybe someone with a goal. I believe that for a while she watched for signs of restraint or control. She may have been a little disappointed to discover that what she looked for was not there in me. She was so sweet and kind, though, that she let me down gently. When Rachel told me she had met someone and couldn't see me any longer, I wasn't hurt or shocked or anything. I couldn't remember what we had in common.

CHAPTER TWENTY ONE

I have had enough of it out here. I turn away from the river and head toward my apartment. The beer in me has gone away with strolling, sweating and time. I am sort of fed up with myself. I wonder what to do to reconcile myself with this life I have fallen into, or rather the one I created. Maybe I need a different life. I could probably do yoga and meditate the rough parts of my mind into more comfortable shapes; shapes with no odd bumps or sharp edges. I don't think that's for me. That would require a lot of time and concentration and there is no guarantee that it would work. I want something that works. It would be easier if the undesirable parts were physical. Then I could find a way to control and rehabilitate them or cut them off and leave the rest. It would be satisfying to simply remove a wretched growth that is at best unsightly, at worst terminal. I picture persistent cancerous cysts that respond momentarily to my attention and then resume the persecution of my conscience as soon as my mind wanders, like tumors on my psyche. Anything that's comfortable or attractive is cornered and harassed by something that's baffling and ugly. But I carry that around with me all of the time and I'm used to it by now. I could carry it back to the bar with me to visit Katrina some more. But I know what going to a bar would accomplish and I don't think it would reconcile anything. The same old anesthetized steps to nothing that go nowhere. Plus, it would cost a bunch of money and, anyway, my social hour is over. I am in a different hour now.

I head down the new canal-walk next to the new hand rail. I feel a sense of determination, but about nothing specific. It's getting late but it's still hot and sunny and I'm still me. A scruffy guy wearing a greasy looking wool cap furiously pushes a shopping cart through the lot. Maybe the cap just looks greasy because it's absorbing the sweat that must be coming out of his scalp. He stops when he draws near me. Jesus. What does he want from me? I am sure that I can guess. It wears on me, the way these guys have no compunction when it comes to approaching someone who is obviously trying to mind his own business; no dignity when asking for a handout from a stranger. Specifically me. I know that I am only a few more mistakes from becoming that guy. Or maybe I am looking in a mirror. But I could never do that. I hate it. But how do I know that I couldn't? I hate a lot of things and I did them. Quite a few of these degenerates are pretty quick to be pissed off if I don't turn them down nicely enough, too. Dirty-cap is one of those. Am I required to explain why I'm not going to give him something? I would rather explain to him what 'fuck off' means. Instead, I have to go through a mini stare-off with him on this late afternoon so that I can prove to him that I see him and I am turning down a real person. Maybe it would be worth giving him money if I got to kick him in the groin or throw him into the canal. Or both. But I don't want to touch him, he's too greasy. But, on second thought, maybe I'm looking at everything wrong and I misunderstand what Dirty-cap and the rest of them want.

I feel the need to change things, to get a handle on them. Suicide is an option, sure, but not the only one and I don't think it's even the best one. Do any of these other stumblebums think about doing everyone a favor and committing suicide? If the city relied on suicide to get rid of all of the undeserving shitheels it would be a truly terrible place. I think it is a matter of courage. None of us have the guts to actually commit the act. We think about it, about how worthless and contemptible our lives have become, and we know the city, the whole world, would be better off without us. We know in our hearts that the right thing, the honorable thing, would be to take ourselves out; to do the deed. None of us can muster up the courage. So Dirty-cap and I aren't going to commit suicide, but that doesn't mean things have to go on like they are. Maybe we all need a little help. I remember the slogan from an environmental group in the old days was that each individual has to commit to doing his or her part to effect change. I think everyone was supposed to recycle. They were trying to save the world. Not me. I will settle for saving my spare change and for going outside without being fucked with. Still, I wouldn't mind doing something helpful and become a contributor to the improvement of the city. I wonder what little thing I could do. I have a vague idea. Once I figure out what my part is, maybe I will commit to it and I will effect change. How could I do my part if I were gone? Though what kind of contribution and what change remain to be seen. I feel it's the hour for focus, for decisions, for action. I try to collect my jumbled thoughts.

I could be continually failing at the things that mean the most because I'm having trouble with my follow-through. It could be that I keep lying to myself and so lying to everyone else. It seems like I've only ever been good for one thing and a good solid relationship isn't it. I'm good at the getting together part, but not the lasting happiness part. Maybe if I committed to something helpful I could get in, do the good deed, and get out before everything turns sour and heart-breaking. I could do something good and actually reach my potential. There must be something. Possibly I just have to do something with certainty, with commitment. Maybe there is a way for me to become valuable again like all of the other formerly useless and forgotten things in this city. Maybe I have some things to make up for. An idea is forming in my head. A way for me to help out may be to lend my courage to those who don't have any of their own. It wouldn't cost anything and the reward might be great. I am headed home to do nothing, but I want to do something. I am determined. If I could fix something or purge something I think I would feel better about existence. Maybe with the right approach and a real commitment I could do something right and make a real improvement for a change. It doesn't have to be a lot; a little improvement is better than none. Rome wasn't built in a day. I could start small by helping one person fix one thing and it would improve everything, the way taking off a scab or cutting off a mole encourages healing. The city has been cleaning up but there are some things it can't do anything about. If I were to believe in signs like some people do, I could take this budding clarity as a sign for me to do my part and clean up just one little thing. If one blemish is removed, it will be a little bit better. I feel that there are some persistent cysts here on the psyche of my adopted city, or the city that has adopted me, and they all know it. Those tormented souls want freedom from a prison of wretchedness as much as everyone wants to be free of them. I feel that they are crying out for relief. I am a little energized because I think I have an idea of how to answer the essential question. I at least have a possibility of where to go from here. Maybe I can be good for something other than the destruction of happy or beautiful things and I can help make something happier or more beautiful instead. I can take away something that makes everything worse. I have been misunderstanding what all of the beggars and bums have been asking me for. I can make some pain, misery and despair go away by giving some assistance. I think they all want it. That's what they have really been asking me for, I just misunderstood.

I walk toward my apartment building. Formerly owned by one of the important and successful textile manufacturing giants that put so many people to work around here, my apartment building was one of those that made Lowell a model of the philanthropic American industrial revolution. The men who owned this gigantic moneymaker of a building, and the giant moneymaking buildings just like it, were so magnanimous that they have gone down in history as the kindly bunch of broad-minded softies that gave all of those unfortunate country girls a life of opportunity and enlightenment. In a mill. Kind of like Ebenezer Scrooge after a bunch of ghosts scared the shit out of him. In the story, Scrooge became very charitable and gave away all kinds of money after the ghosts took him around to show him that everybody would be glad when he was dead. Nobody would miss him because he was such a selfish and greedy bastard. In real life, I don't think Lowell and Appleton and Cabot and Dutton and Boott and Ayer gave anything away. I'm suspicious of the altruistic reputations of the rich and powerful men who made this city great. I'll bet they pretended to be charitable so that they got the recognition as well as the wealth. It could not have been an accident that they all became fabulously wealthy. Those guys named all of the streets after themselves so that while they raked in all of the money from everywhere, everyone could thank them for their generosity. Plus, their names could live on in history, spread around on the historic tours, never to be forgotten. Scrooge should have thought of that. I'll bet a mill girl who was brought here and locked down for the rest of her miserable youth in a manufacturing plant thought of the owners a little differently than benevolent care-takers. I'll bet that the big bosses brought a bunch of girls from out of town to lock down in the mills for more than just their dexterity with bobbins and yarn. Maybe I am just cynical, but in the days before fair labor practices, equal rights and sexual harassment, why didn't those kind-hearted do-gooders hire any males?

CHAPTER TWENTY TWO

Walking through the grounds of my building, I try to avoid the random people in the courtyard. They aren't all tenants. Some are visitors and some are people who find parking near the courtyard so they can walk through to do things in town. There are also homeless bums sometimes walking through. Though it isn't hard to avoid everyone out here, I would like to be invisible now. I keep my head down or turned, like there is something very interesting off to one side, then off to the other. It is quite a nice courtyard, with the uneven block stones making up the yard and smooth paved walk paths running through it. I open the exterior doors with the recognition button on the keys and go to the elevator. Then up to the fourth floor and down the hall to my door. In keeping with the spirit of the city, the building was a dilapidated wreck of an abandoned mill that has been renovated and converted into pretty nice apartments. The mill girls lived in these buildings, too. Well, not this exact one. This was a manufacturing building only, but a lot of us live in it now. Just like the mill girls, sort of. Open and light, it is five stories of new and fresh living in an ideal location just on the edge of downtown. It is on one side of the busy and active DTL where all things are within a couple of blocks. Yet vacant dark lots where other building used to be, and secluded isolated spots near the canal, border our living grounds so intimately that they seem part of the property. There are bright floodlights that illuminate a good bit of the area at night, but there are also some spots that are made even darker in contrast with the lights. In my apartment, I can decide on the answer to the essential question with my new understanding of what everyone needs, wants and asks for every time they see me. Where do I go from here? I go to assist them.

Just like yesterday and the day before that, I could sit for a while and then go to bed. No change. Inaction. Inertia. Stagnation. If I were to continue this way, pretty soon mold would form on my spirit. Maybe more mold. If I let the currents of time and passivity carry me along, tomorrow will come to me. I will have no more understanding of what happened to lead me here, why she sent me away, and why the city adopted me. Tomorrow will come with more of nothing, no improvement, no growth, no nothing unless someone else decides I should do something. Sitting and waiting is not very hard, it doesn't take a lot of energy, but I still don't usually have trouble going to sleep. I have never counted sheep or anything, but once upon a time I used to envision making specific basketball moves to soothe me until I was able to sleep. I made my moves with confidence and skill. Almost always the same ones. It was in the gym on the basketball court during a game. I had the ball up toward the top of the key while the big men tried to run a play down low. I made a ball fake and drove to the right toward the rim. The defender was just a little slow and I beat him by half a step. I took three steps, jumped off my left foot with just the timing and control I wanted. I reached my spot high in the air and gently floated toward the backboard and rim. The helping defender was a little late getting over to attempt the block on my shot and I extended the ball above his outstretched hand. My fingertips were an inch or less from the bottom of the rim as I almost placed the ball on the backboard. I was a little bit too low to dunk it with energy and violence. Instead, in the midst of the frantic action in my fantasy, with defenders closing in to prevent me from reaching the goal, following an explosion of effort and strength and strategy; the court and players and the air frenetic, twirling and hectic as my body absorbed and channeled it. The vibrating energy collected by my flying body, controlled, focused and diminished as it went up the length of my arm until, at the end of my arm, my hand was in perfect control and I lay the ball on the backboard right behind the rim. The ball itself was barely moving when I set it on little square behind the rim to drop down through the net for the score. I used to replay that in my mind over and over, until I was soothed and calmed, finally able to sleep. That fantasy doesn't soothe me these days. Now I envision something else to help me sleep.

I picture myself on a hillside in the woods at dusk. At the bottom of the hill is a rough-edged ravine that makes the place higher up where I am accessible only with a great deal of effort. In my fantasy, I have climbed up the hillside until I am at the edge of a cliff-type platform protected from above by the earth of the hill higher up. It is less than a cave but more than a divot out of the hillside that I crawl into. The only approach to the protected half-cave is up the hillside the way I have already come. I have a wound in my back and I seek silent isolation in this hidden and almost protective place. The wound is a knife stuck in my back about a third of the way down below my left scapula. I don't know where the knife comes from, it doesn't matter. I don't know how I got so far up the hillside with the knife stuck in my back, but that doesn't matter either. People do more difficult things with worse injuries than that. I remember the story of a mountain man in the west during the discovery of America who got mauled by a grizzly bear and was left for dead by his party. Over the course of many weeks with his face and scalp torn apart, broken arm and leg also ripped apart, he made his way hundreds of miles to a settlement and survived. A knife wound isn't such a big thing compared to that. I crawl in and lie on the ground on my side in the recess in the hillside. It hurts quite a lot, but of course, it is a fantasy and I feel no pain at all. In my imagination, I lie there on my side without moving, just breathing. I breathe over and over. I imagine it only once each night. It is soothing.

CHAPTER TWENTY THREE

I'm not ready to go to bed right now. Inaction has never helped me solve or even salvage anything in the past. Maybe it's entropy in disguise and instead of doing nothing I will spin around in a whirlpool of chaos until I disintegrate. Instead of sitting I feel like doing my small part in effecting positive change. With all of the needy asking for so much lately, I know their want is greater than any fatigue of mine anyway. I look at some clothes still lying out from wearing or washing earlier. Nothing really fits right any more, like my body has altered. I have a black t-shirt right there, which fits all right. The pants are sort of baggy now, but that's what belts are for. I have black belts. At night I could be invisible if I were to wear all black. With the right footwear, I could soundlessly glide through the city like a wraith; like one of the ring-wraiths in 'The Hobbit' that only people with special powers can see. If I wore that t-shirt, though, someone could see my arms in the darkness. If I want to be invisible, I want long sleeves. There are dark shirts in the closet, but they are button down shirts and would be unusual around here at night. I don't want to dress up for a prom. No problem. I have a long sleeve black t-shirt in the dresser that Rebecca got for me at a concert. I guess there is no need to keep it in brand new condition. I may as well face the fact that she isn't going to see me wear it. I could put it on inside out so no lettering would show. I also have more than one pair of baggy black pants that are a dull kind of material. Black sneakers and socks, too.

Someone could see my hands and face. I have black gloves that I wore on the motorcycle in my last life. I don't think face-black is good; it would look suspicious. Besides, the only thing I have that would work is some black shoe polish in the cupboard under the kitchen sink. After sitting around under the sink for so long, it's now probably just dried out old wax. I think I could bring it back to life by rubbing it with water or something and make it useful. I don't want to put that on my face anyway. All of the tools remaining from a time when I cared about fixing things are under the sink, too. I have never bothered to throw them in the dumpster or the canal. I have a filet knife that I have never used. I don't even know what I would use it for, never mind why I have it. It should be sharp, though. It doesn't have to be razor sharp, as long as it's sharp enough. It is fairly long, longer than my hand but not as long as my lower arm. Nice. It has a hard plastic sheath too, so it won't cut or poke me if I put it in my pants. I lay it all out and look it over. Yeah. I take off my white shorts and white palm tree shirt from Aruba.

Daytime whites, nighttime blacks. These summer days are pretty long. I like that. It gives me a lot of time to think in the clear light of day. Daylight is for thinking. It will be dusk soon enough and will get dark shortly afterward. I walk around my little apartment cultivating my thoughts. I will make a commitment to improvement and I will maintain focus. The lack of commitment and focus has been my problem. I visualize going out, staying in shadows, looking preoccupied and innocuous. Once I hit the dark area, I will be free to look any other way. I put on the black pants. I have lost enough weight that I have to gather in the waist. My weight loss came because I stopped eating right when I lost my way. I actually stopped eating at all for a while. I sat around in a beach chair wondering what happened, but now I know. I was not committed or focused and I got lost. Losing a bunch of weight has worked out because now I don't stand out by being large. My strength hasn't diminished that much and I am less noticeable or intimidating. It works out also because now these clothes that used to be form fitting have room in them. I have already poked extra holes in the belt but I won't make it tight because I want a little extra space. Black socks and sneakers are good and stealthy for a wraith. I didn't lose any weight from my feet. The long sleeved shirt and gloves nearly cover all of me. I may have found my way at last now that I have focus and commitment. I know where to go from here. Night time has come now. Nighttime is for action. Dressed in my nighttime blacks, I turn off the lights while looking in the mirror. It looks OK, at least in the mirror. I am as invisible as I can probably get. I put the filet knife in my waist under my shirt and belt. I wonder how many people will want something from me. I think that all of us entering the darkness have an agreement with each other. Do they all want me to be myself? Do any of them? If someone asks me for something in the dark places out there, I wonder if I will give him or her what he or she wants. I think I will. I will be a Renaissance man yet. My face is the only white spot that shows in my darkness. I think I can live with that.

Born and raised in Northwood, New Hampshire, Clay Sauls Studied English at the University of New Hampshire and Literature at the University of New Orleans. He currently lives in Lowell, Massachusetts.

Thank you, Wade and Melissa. I couldn't have done it without you.